At the turnoff to the shop he put a hand on my arm and turned me to face him. We stood staring at each other. "You know, Wart, you really ought to talk to your old man. He's just coming on a might too strong." His tone was easy, but the hardness in his eyes betrayed him.

For the first time I saw that Cummings was no taller than I was and I could look him right in the eye. "Really? I don't see what concern it is of yours."

"Well," he drawled, reaching out and slowly starting to turn my top shirt button, "I'm going to make it my concern real quick if the Toad doesn't lay off us."

"Take your hand off my shirt!"

Cummings gave the button a vicious twist and it sprang from my shirt and skittered across the hall. My right fist came up as if it had a mind of its own. Cummings slipped the blow expertly and my fist only grazed the back of his head. A shock just below my rib cage nearly lifted me off my feet and sent the wind exploding from my lungs. A second punch slammed against the side of my head, dropping me limp to the floor.

Wart, Son of Toad

Alden R. Carter

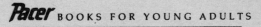

Pacer BOOKS FOR YOUNG ADULTS

BERKLEY BOOKS, NEW YORK

Acknowledgments

I am indebted to my former colleagues and students at Marshfield Senior High School, particularly Walt Chapman, Neil Greebling, and John Bittrich. Thanks also to my sister, Cynthia Carter LeBlanc, Detective Jerry Thieme of the Marshfield Police Department, and my friends Georgette Frazer, Sue Babcock, Gerri Stratton, and Anne Lee. As always, my agent, Ray Puechner; my friends Dean Markwardt and Don Beyer; my wife, Carol; and my editor, Refna Wilkin, were my main sources of emotional support and sound advice.

Wart, Son of Toad is a work of fiction. The resemblance of any character to anyone living or dead is coincidental and should be disregarded.

This Berkley/Pacer book contains the complete
text of the original hardcover edition.

WART, SON OF TOAD

A Berkley/Pacer Book, published by arrangement
with the author

PRINTING HISTORY
Pacer Books edition / October 1985
Berkley/Pacer edition / October 1986

ISBN: 0-425-08885-5

Pacer is a trademark belonging to
The Putnam Publishing Group.

A BERKLEY BOOK ® TM 757,375
Berkley/Pacer Books are published by The Berkley Publishing Group,
200 Madison Avenue, New York, NY 10016.
The name "BERKLEY" and the stylized "B" with design are
trademarks belonging to Berkley Publishing Corporation.

PRINTED IN THE UNITED STATES OF AMERICA

For my mother,
Hilda Carter Fletcher

"Hey, Wart! Hey, Freakman!"

I recognized Vanik's voice and winced. My arms were wrapped around the car battery and the footing was tricky, but I glanced back anyway. In an instant my day went to hell. My feet slipped on a patch of ice and for what seemed like a long second I was in the air. I landed flat on my back, the heavy battery slamming me into the pavement. A cap popped off and went skittering across the ice as acid splashed down the front of my coat.

"Smooth, Wart! Real smooth." Vanik and Cummings were laughing. "Way to go, Wart!"

Keith, the Freakman, grabbed the battery and tipped it upright. "You've got acid all over you, man. Better run and wash it off."

I jumped up, nearly fell again, and ran for the shop, the laughter of the two jocks following me.

"It really wasn't my fault, Dad. I slipped on some ice and fell. I didn't try to spill acid on myself."

"Ya, ya, ya. It wasn't your fault. Why the hell were you carrying that battery anyway?"

All the way home he'd been laying crap on me about the coat. Not that I didn't feel bad enough already. The coat had been new at Christmas, and now two huge holes and a dozen smaller ones were burned in the blue nylon. And Dad was going to make sure I felt just as terrible as possible. I tried to explain again. "I told you why, Dad. My friend's car wouldn't start, so we took the battery into the shop to give it a quick charge. I was just trying to help a friend."

"Is your friend going to pay for your coat?"

"Why should he? It wasn't his fault either."

Dad parked the car in front of the apartment building. "So I'm the one who has to pick up the tab for a seventy-five-dollar coat. Why didn't you leave it inside? It isn't that cold."

Right, I thought. And if you'd seen me outside without a coat in March, you'd have given me hell about that. "I'm sorry, Dad. You don't have to buy me a new coat. I can still wear this one."

"That is not the point, Steven. The fact is that you weren't thinking again and now the damage is done!" He got out and slammed the car door behind him.

I sat for a minute staring at the burns in the front of my soggy coat, then got out and followed him into the building.

Dad had already hung up his coat and gone into the living room to turn on the lamp next to the picture of Mom and my sister, Roxy. I've never known him to forget. It's been almost three years since the car accident, but it's always the first thing he does when we come home. It's like a ritual with him, and that corner table is like a shrine. He'll stand looking at the picture for a few seconds, longer sometimes, then come back to the kitchen to start making supper.

I loved them too, but I don't make a habit of staring at the picture every day. Why torture myself? But I think Dad enjoys the pain, almost as if he's punishing himself. But it wasn't his fault; he wasn't even in the car. Mom and Roxy were coming back from seeing my grandmother in Madison when a truck pulled out in front of them. Bang! No survivors. Just a dead truck driver, a dead mother, and a dead ten-year-old girl. No one to blame—at least no one living.

I hung my coat over a chair in front of a heat vent and began setting the table. Dad started in on me again as soon as he came back into the kitchen. "It would be different if you'd spilled something on yourself in a chemistry class. Why on earth are you taking auto mechanics anyway?"

God, we'd been through this before. "I like it, Dad, and I'm pretty good at it too."

"You could be good at a lot of things if you tried a little harder. You got a B in biology last year." He started making dinner.

I didn't reply, just finished setting the table. I couldn't argue with Dad. He'd simply twist my words to show how I'd failed again. "What else do you want me to do about supper, Dad?"

"Nothing! I can do it alone. Go start your homework." That was standard routine since I brought home lousy grades at semester. While he made dinner, I was supposed to study. But I rarely did. I just brought books home for the sake of appearances.

I slumped into the chair before my littered desk. I really ought to do some algebra, I thought. God, have I fallen behind. Oh, to hell with it. I'll do it after supper before the Bucks game comes on.

I leaned back, thinking. Damn, had the coat thing ever happened at the wrong time. I hadn't told Dad yet, but I planned to sign up for auto mechanics Capstone in the spring. And, boy, was he going to hype out. He still wanted me to make it his way, but I had other ideas. No college for this boy. I didn't want to be a schoolteacher or a doctor or a lawyer. Capstone would give me the training to make it my way. As a junior, I'd spend half my time in vocational classes and, as a senior, I'd only go to school mornings. In the afternoons I'd get credit for working as an apprentice mechanic. By the time I graduated, I'd be a pretty fair wrench-twister. While a lot of the other kids were sweating their butts off in college or trade school, I'd be holding down a job doing what I liked.

But there were two problems: Dad's permission and my grades. I needed a C average to get into Capstone and it looked pretty tight. Sitting staring at my books wasn't helping any either. I opened my American history book and found my place—"Bryan and Free Silver." Who the hell cared? I started reading listlessly.

Dad already had the TV tuned to the game and the announcer was giving the starting lineups. I plopped onto the couch. Time to mellow out. Dad was correcting papers on the coffee table, his red pen gliding down the columns, occasionally striking like a snake to mark an answer wrong. "Done with your homework?" he asked without looking up.

"Most of it."

"Mr. Hoffman said you failed a history exam last Friday."

Damn! So he knew about that already. I'd hoped that Hoffman would keep his mouth shut until I could talk to him. When you're a teacher's kid, everyone expects you to be some kind of genius. I shrugged. "I made a mistake on the essay."

He leaned back and gazed at me through his thick glasses. "A mistake? You don't fail for just making a mistake. He said you didn't even do it."

"I didn't know that chapter was going to be on the test."

"What? Speak up, don't mumble!" I cleared my throat and said it again. "Why didn't you know?" I looked down. "Have you lost that notebook already?"

I'd been dreading this. As part of Dad's latest campaign to get me organized, he'd given me a small assignment notebook to carry. It had lasted about a week before some jocks had started playing catch with it in the locker room. "Hey, look what Wart's got." Toss. "Aw, ain't that cute? Just like his daddy's." Toss. "Come on, guys," I pleaded, trying to intercept it. "Well, ain't that nice? I bet you Wart's going to be a teacher just like the Toad." Toss. "Hey, Fred, ain't you afraid you're gonna get warts touching that?"

"Ugh." Fred, a big lineman on the football team, dropped the notebook. I dived for it, but he kicked it away. One of the other jocks kicked it into the showers. I lunged after it just as my gym teacher, Mr. Lindon, came out of his office. "Hey, Michaels," he yelled at me, "no shoes in the showers." I came back and took them off. Fred stood there laughing. Except for Vanik, he's the worst.

By the time I got to the notebook, it was soaked through and the ink was running on the pages. I threw it in the bottom of my locker and finished getting dressed. Perry Martin, one of the other dirts, as the jocks called us, was combing his long curly hair beside me. His movements were quick and angry and he was muttering. As usual, his best friend, Jeff Kesler, was telling him not to hype out. They were my friends and sympathized with me, but even Perry hadn't been angry or foolish enough to interfere. On the way out of the locker room, I dropped the notebook in a wastebasket.

Now my father, the Toad, sat waiting for me to tell him what had become of the precious notebook. His lips were thin under his sandy mustache and his scowl made the deep lines on his face even deeper. He was tapping his infernal red pen on the chair arm. "Well?"

"Some of the guys were screwing around in the locker room and it got ruined."

"Ruined." He shook his head angrily. "You couldn't hold on to it for two weeks."

"It wasn't my fault."

He gazed at me for a few seconds, then sighed. "It doesn't seem like anything is ever your fault, Steven." I didn't reply. What was the point? He'd just twist my words. He turned back to his work. "Well, notebook or no notebook, you're going to have to get organized. It's almost the end of the third quarter and finals will be here before you know it. You'd better get humping." I didn't say anything, just sat watching the TV. "And I mean tonight!" He glared at me.

I looked into those angry blue eyes and for a second hated him so much that I almost told him where he could shove all his organization. But I didn't. I got up and walked, shoulders slouched, to my room.

I still had the algebra to do, but I sure didn't feel like working on it now. Screw it. I'd copy it from someone in the morning. I flipped disinterestedly through an old hot-rod magazine for a few minutes. Couldn't go out. Couldn't watch TV. Didn't want to do homework. Take a bath. Nothing better to do.

A few minutes later I settled back in the tub and tried to let the hot water relax me. What a bummer this day had turned out to be. Before the battery screwup, it actually hadn't been too bad. Only old lady Rawls had called on me in class. I hadn't known the answer, but she hadn't made a fool of me about it. I'd avoided Dad all day and just two or three kids had given me the Wart treatment. But then Vanik had yelled, "Hey, Wart!" and I'd lost my concentration for a disastrous second.

Wart, son of Toad. It's great to be a teacher's kid, especially when the kids hate your old man. Dad teaches biology and gets about two-thirds of the kids when they're freshmen. He knows his stuff, but he's strict and doesn't have much patience. If a class doesn't get the answer right away or screws up on a test, Dad gives them holy hell. I walk by in the halls some days and hear him just dumping on the kids. He gets going on his "organization" lecture and his "school is your work" lecture, and by the end of the hour those kids are just steaming.

They take it out on him by calling him Toad. He has warts on his hands that he has to get burned off every couple of years. Years ago somebody made the crack that he got them from handling too many toads in his biology class. That didn't make much sense since he uses frogs in biology, but the name stuck.

Dad knows that most of the kids don't like him, and it hurts him a lot. More than just about anything, he wants his students to respect him. And in a lot of ways, they should. He works his butt off teaching. He goes in early, stays late, and brings work home almost every night. But Dad just doesn't have the right personality to be a high-school teacher—not in this century, anyway. Freshman biology is required, and

12

most of the kids hate it. It seems the harder Dad tries to teach the kids something, the more they dislike him.

Dad has put up with the kids' dislike for so long that I think he's forgotten how to be friendly. When a kid smiles at him in the hall and says, "Good morning, Mr. Michaels," he just grunts or mutters, and pretty soon that kid, like most others, looks the other way when meeting him.

But they don't hurt him like the ones who yell, "Hey, Toad!" at his back, then duck around a corner or down a stair. A few have even said it to his face and then all hell breaks loose. Dad isn't a big man, but he's wiry and not above slamming a kid against a locker. I'm worried he's going to get punched out one of these days. Matter of fact, I'm worried he's going to go nuts one of these days. Some nights he comes home wound so damn tight I think he's going to explode. And I have to listen to him. He's got to replay the whole day over and over again, complaining about the kids, complaining about the administration, complaining about the other teachers—just bitch after bitch after bitch.

Actually, I think he does have a real bitch against the administration. After Mr. Quinn quit at the end of last year, they took away Dad's advanced biology course, saying the enrollment was too small—even though Dad had never had more than eight or ten students in the class. That made Dad available to teach more freshmen. Then they took away Mr. Bortz's advanced chemistry course and gave him the rest of the freshman biology sections. Bingo! One less teacher on the payroll.

It was a lousy trick, because Dad really loved that advanced class. He'd move from table to table, smiling and kidding with the kids. Most of them were seniors planning to major in biology or premed in college. Dad could talk to them and work with them on more than the basics. And those kids usually liked Dad too. Some of them still send Christmas cards or call him up when they're in town. Dad is real proud of some of them who've made it pretty big by this time. And I

13

guess he wishes I was more like them. But I'm not. I want to be a mechanic, not a doctor or a biologist. I got a B last year only because I worked pretty hard for Mr. Quinn, who was a good guy and gave me a break or two. I wish he hadn't quit to take a job with the government. Dad is even harder to live with now.

When Dad gets done complaining about things at school, he starts in on me. I can't remember a night recently when we haven't argued about something: my hair, my clothes, my studies, my friends—there's always something. Maybe we wouldn't fight so much if Mom were still around. Before the accident I don't remember fighting with Dad. Maybe we were different then, or maybe we just didn't have much to fight about. After all, I was a lot younger. Now I figure I've got some rights and can make my own choices—like with the Capstone thing. But the rules say I have to have Dad's permission. Bummer.

It particularly irks Dad that I hang around with dirts. But they at least have the decency not to call me Wart all the time. My nickname is more recent than Dad's. A pretty girl named Melissa was the first to call me Wart. That was back in eighth grade, and I remember that day just as well as yesterday, maybe better. I'd had a crush on her all fall and was trying to get up the nerve to ask her to go to the movies. So, I was pretty excited when she and her friend Karen sat down across from me at lunch.

"My brother's got a Mr. Michaels for biology. Is that your Dad?" Melissa asked. I nodded, feeling my insides start to churn. I'd been through this before—a lot of kids had older brothers and sisters in Dad's classes. "Tom says none of the kids like him. They call him Frog." They both giggled.

"Toad," I said. "They call him Toad."

"Same difference. Why do they call him that?"

I explained about the warts.

"Ich," Karen said, "my great-aunt's got warts. I think they're gross. Do you have warts too?"

I shook my head.

14

Melissa's eyes started shining. "Hey, if they call him Toad, maybe we should call you Wart."

My stomach flipped over. I tried to say something, but it was already too late. They were giggling so hard that several other kids asked them what the joke was. As I stammered, Melissa repeated her inspiration, and soon a lot of kids were laughing and calling me by my new nickname. Like a dumb ass, I jumped up and ran out of the cafeteria. I cried in a stall in the bathroom. The name would stick, I knew it.

And it did. When I got out of junior high, I hoped it would get left behind. There were two junior highs in town, so half the freshmen and most of the older kids wouldn't know the Wart. No such luck. By the middle of my freshman year, hardly anyone except the teachers seemed to be using my real name. That's about the time I started to hang out with the dirts. People were already dumping on them and I figured I'd be right at home with the school's other misfits. Jeff and Perry had already drifted into the group. I'd asked them not to call me Wart and they told the other guys I didn't like it. Some of them forget now and then, but I hear it less often from dirts. I'm not really a hard-core dirt. Dad would never let me grow my hair very long or wear my coat all the time, but I stay on the fringe of the group and feel more or less accepted.

I don't know why some kids become dirts. Some are just born rebels, I guess. Like Perry. Even when he was a little kid he had a chip on his shoulder. I think he always resented being smaller than most kids his age. He started lifting weights in junior high and that made him pretty tough, but he just never got over being small. Sometimes he seems to go out of his way to get in trouble.

He'd get in a lot more if it wasn't for Jeff, who's pretty calm and keeps Perry cool most of the time. Jeff is fairly straight for a dirt and keeps up in his studies. Like a few of the others he sees himself as a modern-day hippie or beatnik or something. He's into music and art and even tries to write poetry. He's only so-so at those things, but he's a good guy and we humor him.

Keith and some of the others are harder to figure out. They just seem to have said to hell with everything. If Keith had a different attitude, he could probably be one of the stars of the school. He's real smart and I think he could ace any course if he tried. He's about six-three and probably could have played on the basketball team too. But Keith doesn't give a damn about sports or schoolwork or much of anything: I think his lousy home life has a lot to do with it. His parents are big drinkers and his dad can get real mean. I've seen Keith come to school more than once with a cut lip or a bruised cheek. He says even less than usual those days and he's usually stoned by the end of school.

Keith does a lot of drugs and they make him quiet and distant. I wish he'd talk to me more about his problems, but one of the reasons we get along is that I don't ask too many questions. He had a girl when I first met him, but he dumped her. I asked why one afternoon and he looked at me for a long moment before he said, "She was trying to get inside my head all the time. I don't like that." I got the hint.

On the average, dirts drink more, smoke more, skip more classes, and study less than most kids. But there's more going on than just trying to have a good time. There's a lot of anger among the dirts. They resent a system that rewards kids who just happen to be born athletic or musical or smart, while ignoring all the rest. Most kids just go along with that, but dirts make a point of showing their anger with long hair, sloppy clothes, and a don't-give-a-damn attitude. And there are the drugs too. Not that a lot of the jocks and "good kids" don't get stoned; dirts are just more obvious about it.

Even more than the administration and the teachers, the dirts hate the jock crowd. Not every kid who goes out for a sport is a jock. Some play on school teams and then go on about their business. The real jocks are the ones who make a point of showing how superior an athletic letter makes them. The jocks like to throw their weight around and the dirts are easy targets. The dirts hate them for the abuse and because the jocks can get away with stuff that would get dirts in deep trouble real fast. The jocks figure that they don't have to obey rules, and the administration and a lot of the teachers seem to agree with them. But not Dad, and he's had a lot of run-ins with the jocks. They make a point of telling me.

Dad rapped on the bathroom door. "Are you going to stay in there all night?" His voice was irritable.

"Just getting out." I grabbed the soap and washed quickly. I could hear him walking around, straightening up. We live in a two-bedroom apartment and Dad is always cleaning up. "If we don't keep it clean," he's fond of saying, "we'll smother in our own garbage." He's right on that score, I guess, but he's a fanatic about it, always yelling at me, even if I just leave the newspaper spread out on the couch or an empty glass on the table.

I dried off and headed for my room with a towel wrapped around my waist. I was getting on my pajamas when he yelled from the bathroom, "Steven, when I'm going to take a bath, I don't expect to have to clean up your muck."

Damn! Forgot to clean the tub again. "Sorry, Dad, I'll get it in a minute."

"Never mind! I can do it faster myself."

That's another one of Dad's favorite lines. He's got a lot of them: "If you'd only done . . ." or "If you'd only listen for once . . ." or, of course, "If you'd only get organized . . ."

I got in bed, turned out the light, and tried to think about something else. Almost the middle of March. Two and a half months left in the school year. That helped a little, but not much. There was still tomorrow.

2

I wrenched free of the dream and sat up. Pitch dark. I took a half-dozen slow, deep breaths. The clock beside my bed said two. Damn. How long would it take me to get back to sleep this time? I wrapped a blanket around my shoulders and looked out the window, waiting for the last of the dream to fade. A heavy wet snow was falling—another dreary morning ahead.

I let the curtain drop and lay back in bed. This had been the first bad dream in quite a while. In the first couple of years after the accident, I'd had them night after night. I'd dream about the gray man and the big uniformed cop who came to tell Dad about the accident. Mom and Roxy would be there in the living room with Dad while I watched from the top of the stairs. Mom, Dad, and Roxy would listen to the gray man and then Mom would smile and say, "Get your coat, Roxanne; we've got to go now." At the top of the stairs I'd try to yell, but I could never get any words out. And Dad would sit there like a stone while Mom and Roxy left with the gray man and the big cop.

The one about the burial was even worse. All sorts of people would be standing around on that little hill in the cemetery while the minister prayed by the freshly dug graves. Then Mom and Roxy would leave the crowd on the other side of the graves and climb into their caskets. Mom would smile at me as she lowered the lid. I'd try to tell her not to go, but no words would come out. I'd turn to tell Dad to stop them, but he'd be standing a long way off, scowling at the scene.

I used to have both dreams a lot—and quite a few others too—but I'd trained myself to wake up at the first sign of trouble. Losing sleep was better than dreaming. But the dream tonight had caught me off guard. It had been a very good dream at first. I'd been far away from Brandt Mills and happy.

I'd been on a river. We were moving very fast, but I felt completely in control. The canoe paddle in my hands was unbelievably light, and I made the steering strokes effortlessly. We shot through an opening between two big rocks and cut back across the river to take a big chute. In the front seat Keith was laughing. Not his bitter laugh, but really laughing. We plunged down the chute and even in my dream I could feel the canoe rear over the rolling wave below. Then we were in quiet water. I looked back to watch Perry and Jeff coming through the rapids. In the bow of their canoe, Perry was drinking a beer while Jeff placidly fished from the stern. The canoe must have had an autopilot, because it was making all the right moves.

But when I turned to say something to Keith, Dad was there instead and he started yelling about "those boys not paying attention" and how they should "get organized." Then he said, "Let's get going. Your mother and sister are waiting." Up ahead on the riverbank I saw them standing by the Buick, and my paddle suddenly weighed a ton. That's when I tore myself from sleep and opened my eyes to the darkness in my room.

Hell, if I kept replaying bad dreams, I'd never get back to sleep. Think about something good, like the real canoe trip Jeff, Perry, Keith, and I had taken in June. I smiled, remembering. Ya, that had been one hell of a good time. The Fearless Four against the wilderness. It had been a wonder we'd survived. I'd been chosen the leader on the strength of a single week's experience on a Boy Scout canoe trip. I'd chosen a section of river without too many rapids and done a lot of praying.

We didn't call ourselves the Fearless Four for long. What a bunch of terrified fools we must have looked like in that first small rapids. We'd been yelling instructions at one another, bouncing off rocks, coming close to turning over a half-dozen times. Still, we'd made it and I took pride in the fact that, despite all the confusion, I'd led us through.

With a little practice and a lot more caution, we got pretty good in the next couple of days. The weather was beautiful. There were no jocks, parents, or teachers to hassle us. We smoked a little grass, drank some beer, caught a few fish, and just mellowed out on the river and nature. I couldn't remember ever being happier.

Back in Brandt Mills, the rest of the summer had been a bummer. Dad was teaching summer school and was as ornery as a constipated bear. He'd insisted that I take typing during the second summer session: "You'll have to know how to type when you get to college." I tried to explain that I didn't want to go to college, but he wouldn't listen to any arguments.

I hated that typing class. At first I thought it might not be so bad, since most of the students were girls and there might be some prospects. But I felt awkward when most of them picked up the typing right away. In two weeks everyone was blasting along while I was still trying to keep the first row straight. Typing wasn't at all like fixing something with your hands. I mean, when you're working on a carburetor or something, you're not expected to read the repair manual at the same time.

At first the girls just teased me a little, but then Cummings, Vanik, and a couple of the other jocks started showing up to hustle some of the girls during breaks. They got the Wart crap going again. Soon the teasing from some of the girls got mean. Not much to do about it except lie low and try to last out the rest of the course.

In the late afternoons, I tried to make a few bucks cutting lawns. Our old beater lawn mower gave up in early August,

20

and after a couple of days working on it, I had to admit it was shot. I was attached to that mower, too. In the summer after Mom and Roxy's death, it had become my friend. I'd taught myself a lot fixing the engine, and cutting lawns kept my mind off the past. But the engine was beyond help and I had to spend all my money and borrow more from Dad to buy a new mower. It took the rest of the summer to get caught up.

When summer school finally got out, I hoped Dad and I could have some fun. We'd at least tried the first two summers after the accident. We'd gone to the movies and softball games. Several times we'd driven to Minneapolis for Twins games and to visit Uncle Jerry's family. Best of all, we'd gone fishing a few weekends. But this summer was different. Uncle Jerry and Aunt Mary had separated in the spring and Dad didn't want to go to Minneapolis and have to listen to their marital problems. At one time he'd suggested that we visit Mom's sisters and their families in St. Louis. But later he'd changed his mind. When I'd asked why, he'd said, "We don't have enough money, Steven, and there are some other things you wouldn't understand." He wouldn't explain beyond that and it wasn't until I stopped one day to look at Mom and Roxy's picture that I thought I understood: he didn't want to be with anyone who reminded him of Mom.

I'd at least hoped that we might get away for some fishing, but after a single trip, he wasn't in the mood for that either. When I suggested going again, he growled, "You need to cut a lot of lawns to pay for that expensive mower." So I cut lawns and he spent most of the time at school preparing for the coming year.

Without a driver's license, money, or a girl, even the nights were a drag. Most of my friends were gone or busy. Things had gotten real bad around home for Keith and he'd gone to Milwaukee to live with an uncle and work in a grocery store. Jeff was off on a long vacation and Perry was working afternoons and evenings.

Starting school again was almost a relief. I figured things would have to be better now that I was a sophomore and knew some of the ropes. I'd be sixteen in October and could get a driver's license at last. Wheels—more freedom and a better sex life. God knows, there hadn't been much of either before.

Trish was my first big opportunity—or so I thought. I was pushing the mower home on a warm Saturday afternoon in September. About a half a block from the apartment building, a Ford station wagon was pulled over to the curb with steam rising from its grille. I recognized the short girl with the top-heavy figure who was trying to find the hood release. I started walking faster.

I'd sat near Trish in freshman English, and although I'd barely known her, she'd always had a smile and a "Hi" for me. That didn't make me anybody special, since she was friendly to everyone. Still, I'd appreciated it and had hoped to get a chance to know her better, maybe even ask her out. "Hi, Trish. What's the problem?"

She glanced up. I could see she was angry almost to the point of tears. "Oh, hi. I can't get the stupid hood open."

"Let me try." I found the release and lifted the hood. A cloud of steam billowed out of the engine compartment, and I stepped back.

"Oh, darn! I must have done something to the car. Dad's going to kill me."

"I don't think it was anything you did. Just a broken hose. It happens." I waved steam away. "There it is." I pointed to an inch-long break in the hose running from the radiator to the block.

"Is it serious?"

"No, just a few bucks."

"Can I drive it home?"

"I wouldn't. It's losing water pretty fast and you could overheat the engine. Then you'd really have problems."

"Darn. Dad's out of town and Mom doesn't have a car. I guess I'll have to call a garage and have them send somebody to fix it."

"You don't have to do that. We can walk downtown and buy a hose. I can fix this in fifteen minutes."

"Could you really?"

"Sure, simplest thing in the world."

"That'd be great!" For the first time she smiled. "I just got my license last week and I hate to bring home a big repair bill so soon."

"I just live over there. Let me put the mower away and we'll go buy the hose."

On the walk to the parts store, she asked me about my summer and I told her a bit about the canoe trip. She said she'd done some canoeing while working at a girls' camp up north near Minocqua. She started talking about the camp and all the funny things that had happened. I didn't say much, just laughed at her stories and enjoyed the feeling of walking beside her. The summer had done her good. She'd lost a few pounds and had a beautiful tan. Maybe she wasn't beautiful, but then I couldn't pass myself off as any movie star.

We bought the hose and walked back to the apartment. I ran in for a few tools, a drain pan, a pair of gloves, and a gallon of hot water.

The engine was still pretty hot and I had to work carefully. She watched. "You know a lot about cars, huh?"

"Not really, but I'm in auto mechanics this year and learning a lot more. I want to be a mechanic after I graduate."

"Oh? I'd have thought you'd want to be a teacher or something."

I laughed and shook my head. "Uh-uh. You can have all that stuff. The sooner I'm done with school, the better."

"I'm thinking about being a dental technician. Or, I don't know, maybe a nurse or something." She talked about that while I worked. I finished getting in the new hose and refilled the radiator.

"Why does the water have to be hot?"

"It probably doesn't, but I don't want to take a chance on cracking the block. Just a safety precaution. There. I think you're ready to roll."

"Gee, thanks, Steve. This has really been great of you."

"My pleasure."

23

We stood for a couple of seconds. Come on, Wart, ask her out, I told myself. Before I could get up my courage, she asked, "Are you going on the cookout tomorrow night with the church youth group."

"I haven't really thought about it. I've only been to one meeting."

"That's okay. I don't go very often myself. They're trying to get more kids involved."

I hesitated. "I don't know. I'm not much for church stuff."

"Oh, you ought to come. It'll be fun." She got in the car. "A bunch of us are going. Should we pick you up?"

"Ya, do that."

She told me what time, thanked me again, and drove off.

I felt wonderful. I mean, she'd sort of asked me out, hadn't she? I could hardly wait for the next evening.

My fantasies about getting close to Trish the next night didn't work out worth a damn. Her station wagon was packed with kids when she picked me up, and I didn't get a chance to talk to her. At the cookout a pretty good-looking guy from Marston, a little town up the road fifteen miles, took up with her right away. Soon they were sitting close and I could tell Trish was really enjoying his attention. Out of luck again, Wart.

I tried to talk to some of the other kids. Wouldn't you know it, a couple of freshmen in Dad's biology classes recognized me and started asking why Dad was such a hard ass. I got out of that discussion as fast as I could and began wishing the stupid cookout was over.

It was getting pretty dark and some of the kids went out to scrounge some more wood for the fire. Trish and the guy from Marston went off together. I headed in the opposite direction, brought back an armful of wood, and went out for another. When I was coming back, I spotted Trish coming in my direction. She had her arms folded and her head down. Sue Christensen and Ellen Hanson were following her. Sue called, "Trish, wait up. What happened?" Trish shook her head and kept walking. I took a couple of steps into the shadows. Sue caught up with Trish and took her by the arm. "Tell me, Trish."

"He mauled me! We were talking and gathering up some sticks and then, bang, he was all over me! Put a lip-lock on me and went straight for my boobs. I tried to push him away, but he wouldn't let me go."

Sue said, "You should have kicked him in the balls."

"I tried, but he had me almost off the ground. God, is he strong! I got him in the shins a couple of times and he pushed me down. Then I bit his hand really hard. He let go and I ran."

Ellen said, "Well, let's go tell the pastor."

"No! I don't want anyone to know. They'll figure I led him on." There was a pause and I heard Trish sniff. "Oh, darn, he even tore a button off my new blouse. I mean, he went right for my boobs. Didn't try to work up to it or anything. Most guys I've gone out with try sooner or later, but not like that."

Sue laughed and said, "Most guys. Well, at least you've got guys asking you out. I wish I had a pair of boobs like yours. Then maybe somebody'd ask me out once in a while."

Trish blew up at that. "God, are you stupid, Sue! I'll trade with you anytime. Then you can have the back pain and sweat like a pig when it's hot. And you can find out how much fun it is to have people staring at your boobs all the time and guys trying to grope you every chance they get." She started to cry.

Ellen said, "Okay. Okay. Calm down, Trish."

Sue said, "Hey, I'm sorry, Trish. I was just trying to make a joke." They moved away and I couldn't hear any more. After a few minutes I made my way back to the fire. The guy from Marston and a couple of his buddies were gone. I was embarrassed for overhearing. And I felt sorry for Trish. Hell, I'd treat her decent. In a few days maybe I'd give her a call.

And I did. She was polite, but said she was busy. I tried again right after I got my driver's license. She'd said okay that time, sounding enthusiastic enough, I thought. But her mood was different when I picked her up. She was polite, but cool—not the cheerful Trish I'd expected. That threw me off right away. Maybe it was nothing. Maybe she'd just had a tough day.

We went to a dance, and a dozen kids must have called me Wart. We sat with some kids I barely knew and right away they started asking me why Dad was such a hard ass. By the time we left, I was so embarrassed I couldn't think of much to say and I guess she couldn't either. It wasn't much of an evening for Trish.

I wanted to try again, but the next time I called she said, "Steve, I'm sorry, but I'm just not looking for a relationship right now. I'd rather just have you as a friend, okay?"

What could I say. I mumbled something and we said good-bye. Damn. And I'd thought I'd really had a chance with her. From what I could tell, she wasn't going out with anyone steady. What was wrong with me? Maybe the old Wart wasn't the best example of handsome and suave young manhood, but he wasn't exactly the creeping pits either. To hell with it. Look around for someone else.

But I didn't find anyone else for anything approaching a relationship. I asked out quite a few girls, but even when one did say yes, it never lasted more than a date or two. Most of it was probably me, but after a while I began to wonder if my connection with Dad had something to do with it. Girls probably thought about the amount of crap they might take for going out with the Toad's son. Was anything the Wart had to offer worth risking social suicide? That probably sounds pretty paranoid, but I've got evidence. Hell, I even asked out Sue Christensen, who had a lot more problems than no knockers, and she'd said no. Twice, for God's sake.

I groaned. Damn. You can't spend all night worrying about it, Wart. Get some sleep. Tomorrow is going to be rough enough as it is. I rolled onto my side and tried to make my mind a blank. It took a long time.

3

Dad cooked breakfast while I set the table. Snow was still falling past the window, a wet, late-winter snow that didn't make anything look better, just added another couple of inches to all the dirty, icy snow waiting for the spring thaw. At least spring was something to look forward to. It had been a long winter; they always are in western Wisconsin, and everyone gets pretty worn down by this time of year. Everyone, that is, except Dad, who's the same year round. He hardly ever smiles and never wavers. Go straight ahead, stay organized, do your job. He was different when Mom and Roxy were alive. I guess I was too, but that's all a long time ago. Now they're just faces in a picture.

Dad put eggs and sausage in front of me. He's not talkative in the morning, thank God, so I usually get off to school without a lecture. On the ride over he'll sometimes give me a pep talk, but usually he's so wound up thinking about the day, he doesn't even do that. Still, going into school with him is a bummer, since a lot of kids see us together. I like spring and fall when I can walk or ride my ten-speed and he drives in alone. In the winter, I try to catch a ride home with one of the guys. That gives me an hour or so by myself before Dad comes chugging home in the Buick.

Dad was in a hurry this morning. "Finish up quick. I've got to get there early to set up a film, and the roads look slippery. We'll leave the dishes until tonight."

That's not like Dad, since he usually insists on cleaning up before school, but I didn't say anything, just bolted my food and went for my light spring coat. Dad had already thrown my ruined winter coat in the garbage—"No son of mine is going to walk around looking like a bum. And get a haircut this week."

Outside I hunched my shoulders against the wind and waited for him to unlock the Buick. The car is a dog, six years old with no pickup and a bad ping. Maybe it doesn't exactly chug, but damn close to it. Back in the fall, I'd suggested taking it into the shop, where the class could fix it up a little, but Dad just snickered. "It'll be a cold day in the hereafter when I let a bunch of kids fix my car. Probably put the valves in upside down."

I don't think Dad knows a valve from a muffler. He can drive a car okay, but he hasn't the foggiest idea what goes on under the hood. That's the one subject I know better than he does, but he won't admit it. So I've given up trying to tell him that the car needs work. I just ride along and try not to grimace when the Buick stalls at a light and the cars behind start honking.

Auto mechanics is about the only thing that keeps me sane at school. The guys in the shop don't hassle me and Mr. Ohm is a good guy. He doesn't say much unless he has to; he'd rather show you, and there's no doubt he knows how to fix cars. I'm no whiz at it, but I can solve a problem with a little thought and I don't mind getting my hands dirty. I find more peace when my hands are working on an engine than at any other time. If it wasn't for auto mechanics every second day, I couldn't make it. And if I could get into Capstone, I'd have it or a related course every day.

We drove the ten blocks to school in silence. Most of the streets hadn't been plowed yet. Brandt Mills is only about 25,000, but it's spread out and it takes a long time for the plows to get around. I was glad Dad was behind the wheel. After I'd gotten my driver's license, I'd usually drive to school, but Dad's constant criticism made me so nervous that we almost had a couple of accidents. Finally, I gave up and let him drive most mornings. Less aggravation for both of us.

As we turned into the faculty parking lot, Dad spoke. "Grades are due tomorrow. Going to get any D's?"

"Couple, I guess."

"What in?"

"History and algebra. Nothing I can't make up. No big deal."

He glared at me. "What do you mean, 'no big deal'? Don't you ever want to graduate, young man?"

"I told you, it's no big problem. They're D's, not F's." He had the car parked and I hopped out before he could say any more. "See you later," I called.

Inside the building I hurried past the office and down the hall. There weren't too many kids in school yet. We'd beaten the buses and most of the kids with their own cars were still on the way or sitting in the parking lot having a last smoke and listening to the radio. Sometimes I'd go out there and find a warm, friendly car, but today I had to find someone with that algebra. I'd been pushing my luck pretty hard recently and I'd have to get my act together pretty fast to make the C average I needed for Capstone.

I'd lied to Dad about my grades. (Not that the lying bothered me. Hell, we were long past that.) Algebra was nearer an F than a D, and history wasn't much better. I hadn't mentioned English to Dad, since I might still get a C— if I could sweet-talk old lady Rawls. Show her I was concerned and she might have a little mercy. I'd played that one on her before, though, and she might not buy it this time. Algebra first. I'd see if Trish was in her homeroom. She'd let me copy hers. Besides, that would give me a chance to be close to her for a few minutes.

I was coming around a corner fast when I almost ran into Mr. Mattson, my speech teacher. He's a small man with a big round stomach that doesn't shake and thin black hair plastered down on his big head. He wears a huge black beard that covers his cheeks, chin, and about six inches of the front of his shirt. Add piercing blue eyes and a sarcastic wit and he could scare Dracula out of his shorts.

"Oh, excuse me, Mr. Mattson," I choked.

"Mr. Michaels, I've been wanting to talk to you. Where were you yesterday? Your name wasn't on the absentee list."

"Gee, I'm sorry. I was going to come and talk to you about that. I went down to the shop during study hall and forgot about class."

"Forgot? You've been around here almost two years, Mr. Michaels. You should be able to keep track of your schedule by now."

I tried to sound as meek as possible. "I'm sorry. I just forgot."

He riveted me with those eyes for what seemed like a minute, then sighed. "Well, come along. I want to give you the assignment."

He led the way toward his office. I still had to get that algebra done. "Uh, Mr. Mattson, I've got something kind of important to do right now. Could I see you later this morning?"

He whirled. "Now look, Mr. Michaels! You want to pass my class, don't you? I don't have time to chase you all over the school. Come now or forget about it."

"Yes, sir." I followed, watching the backs of his shoes.

His office is up in the administration wing, since he's filling in for the assistant principal this year, while Mr. Kirkland is back in college working on his doctorate or something. So Mattson only teaches speech and spends the rest of the time handling discipline. He's good at it. Too good. He changed the detention program so it's got a lot more bite now. For minor stuff you still get study detention and have to sit in a study hall after school. But if you're guilty of something bigger or keep getting caught for minor stuff, Mattson assigns work detention. The janitors always give the work detention kids the crappiest jobs: scrubbing urinals, cleaning walls, moving around heavy boxes of books, and so on. The kids hate the program so much that discipline really has been better this year—or at least kids are more careful not to get caught.

Despite the fact that Dad is heavy on discipline too, he and Mattson don't get along very well. Mattson's strict, but Dad is Stone Age. Dad thinks the school ought to be run the old-fashioned way with a hair and dress code, no smoking on school grounds, and more required courses—and that's just for starters. So while all the kids bitch about how tough things are this year, Dad complains about how loose discipline is. I hear it almost every night.

I stood in the doorway as Mattson dug around in his file cabinet for a copy of the assignment sheet. He put it on the desk and gestured me over. It was a simple assignment, just a five-minute demonstration speech due on Monday, but he insisted on reading most of the instructions aloud, as if I couldn't read myself. I stood there nodding and wishing he'd get done so I could find Trish. But he kept me in his office until the bell for homeroom rang and I had to run to make it before announcements.

Mr. Hoffman gave me a glare as I slid into my seat. What a day this was turning out to be. I got my algebra out and tried to do a couple of the problems while the Phantom—Mr. Severson, the principal—read the announcements over the speaker system. The kids call him the Phantom because we rarely see him in the halls and then he has a funny, fixed smile and eyes that don't seem to focus on anyone. Dad says he's just a politician and a paper-pusher, but Dad hasn't exactly been objective since losing his advanced biology class

The Phantom droned on about club meetings and sports practices. I'd never gone out for a sport and I didn't belong to any clubs either, so I really didn't need to listen. But I felt Hoffman's eyes on me and closed the book. To hell with it, too late to do anything about algebra anyway.

I flunked the pop quiz at the beginning of the hour. I wrote my name at the top of the paper, took one look at the problem, and put my head down on my arms. If this hadn't finished me for the quarter, nothing would. Miss Thomas walked toward my side of the room and I sat up and started doodling with the problem. She walked back, tapping a long wooden pointer on the tiles.

After we handed in the papers, I sat through the rest of the hour trying to be inconspicuous. When the bell rang, she was halfway through picking up the assignments. I made for the door, but she caught me. "Steve, may I have your assignment, please?"

Miss Thomas is just a couple of years out of college and she's easier to fool than most of the older teachers, but I still had a twinge of guilt lying to her. "I forgot it in my locker."

"Well, bring it to me this morning."

"Ya, okay."

I hadn't read the assignment for English, so again I tried to fade into the background, hoping old lady Rawls wouldn't remember that I'd blown a question the day before. Luckily, the bright kids, bless them for a change, volunteered all the answers, and I wasn't called on at all.

Dodging through the crowd in the halls, I began to feel better. The morning was more than half over. Just a study hall and then lunch. We'd get our tests back in history and start a new unit, so I didn't have to worry about a quiz there. Then two hours of auto mechanics and the day would be over. Not too bad as long as the kids didn't get on me with the Wart crap.

No such luck. When I came into the cafeteria for study hall, a bunch of the jocks started giving it to me right away. "Hey, Wart, why was Mattson yelling at you this morning?" It was Tom Vanik again. He rides me more than any of them and he's good at it. I hate him, but it's dangerous to ignore him. Vanik is into violence and even beating the crap out of people in football and wrestling doesn't give him enough.

"Nothing. Just missed a class."

"Well, why didn't you tell him to kiss off? The Toad's kid don't have to take crap from nobody."

Fred and three or four of the other jocks laughed.

"That's right, Wart." Jim Cummings, the quarterback,

leaned back, rocking his chair, cowboy hat tilted back on his head. "You can't go around shivering in your boots. Ya gotta stand up for your rights."

I grinned weakly, but he wasn't smiling. What the hell is going on? I thought. This isn't like Cummings. Vanik, yes— that s.o.b. is always mean—but not Cummings.

Cummings is the school hero. He moved to Brandt Mills a couple of years ago from a little town in Wyoming and likes to be called Cowboy and talk with an exaggerated Western drawl. But on the football field he's not playacting. He's got a passing arm like a rifle and he led the team to the conference championship this year. Around school he accepts the hero's role with lazy good humor. He doesn't do too well in his studies, but even the teachers seem to admire him. In a way, I guess I do too. He's got a ton of talent and charisma—and the prettiest girl in the school. Nice life. He can afford to be good-natured about things.

But now he was watching me with a cold stare. A couple of the other guys tried to get in digs, but Cummings waved for silence. "Tell me, Wart, where does your old man get off? Did he swallow the student handbook or something?"

"Why, what happened?" My voice was a little faint and I cleared my throat.

"The Wart's a little nervous," Vanik grinned.

"Shut up, Tom," Cummings said. (Vanik would have laid out anyone else for saying that.) "Tom and me and some of the guys were playing buckets this morning and the ball hit the door a couple of times." He gestured toward the long line of doors between the cafeteria and field house. "Your old man came through there like a dog with his tail on fire and started yelling about us disturbing the study hall. That was a lot of crap, but he wouldn't listen. Told us to go to the showers and him not even a gym teacher." Oh, God, I thought, Dad's really getting into it now. Cummings' drawl got soft and dangerous. "Now, your old man is getting a lot of guys pretty pissed off. Somebody better tell him to lay off."

"Really, guys, I can't talk to him either."

"Hmmp." Cummings put his feet on an empty chair and tilted his hat over his eyes. "Well, somebody better . . . or watch out."

"Hey, get to work, you guys," one of the study-hall supervisors yelled from a couple of tables away.

I was saved. Teachers could be useful now and then. I hurried off, looking for someone from my algebra class. No luck, so I sat down with Keith and some of the other dirts at a table near the doors to the smoking lounge.

We've got what they call a liberal high school. The kids don't have to smoke in the bathrooms, but can go outside into a small courtyard called the smoking lounge. It gets damned cold in the winter, but there's no hassle if you want a cigarette during the day. Of course, a lot of grass gets smoked out there too, and sometimes one of the supervisors gets brave and raids the smoking lounge, but that's not very often.

Sitting at the table, I should have been doing my algebra, but I was too nervous. I wanted a cigarette, but I'd left my pack in my coat. "Hey, Keith, bum me a cigarette." Keith dug in his pocket and rolled a Marlboro over to me. "Thanks, I'll catch you later."

Keith nodded and went back to studying his long thin hands. Stoned again, I thought. God, I wish he'd ease up on those reds. Maybe I ought to take a chance and talk to him about it. Just say, "Hey, look, man, I'm not trying to get inside your head or anything, but, well, I think you're doing too many downers."

I owed him that. After all, he'd gone out of his way to be my friend. I'd hardly known him until one day in the fall of my freshman year when I'd come to the table pretty upset after some jocks had been giving me the Wart crap. He'd looked up and said in his quiet voice, "Screw 'em, Steve. Forget it." He hadn't said any more, but I'd been grateful for that. At least somebody half-understood.

I'd been walking home the next afternoon when Keith and

his girl pulled up in his battered Chevy. "Need a lift?" he called.

"Sure." I got in next to Barb, a tall, pretty girl .I'd seen around.

"Where do you live?" Keith asked. I told him. "That's on my way. Let me drop off Barb first."

Barb turned to me. "Hey, you're the Toad's son, ain't you? They call you Wart, or something, right?"

"He doesn't need that crap, Barb. His name is Steve."

"Okay, Steve. But your Dad's the Toad, right?"

"Jesus," Keith muttered.

I admitted that Dad was the Toad and Barb started rattling on about having Dad for a teacher the year before and what a hard ass he'd been. Fortunately, she only lived three or four blocks from school, so I didn't have to listen to her for long.

After we let her off, Keith said, "Don't pay any attention to her. Woman has diarrhea of the mouth."

"It's okay," I said.

We were about halfway to the apartment house when Keith said, "Hey, do you want to do a joint, man?"

"Sure."

"Good. Let's drive up to the cemetery."

That was about the last place in the world I wanted to go, but I didn't say anything. Keith drove up the long hill onto the bluff above town. The newer part of the cemetery is on the back side of the bluff. By following the twisting drive between the plots, you can get back to the old section high atop the bluff. The view from there is pretty spectacular for this part of the world. If the day is clear and the smoke from the mill isn't too heavy, you can follow the course of the river for miles after it clears the edge of town to flow through the rich farmland to the south.

We smoked the joint in the car and then got out to sit on the hood and enjoy the view. Keith stretched. "Good place to get high. If someone hassles us, we can just tell them we're visiting somebody's grave."

"I don't think they could argue. My mom and sister are buried over there." I pointed to the small hill in the newer part of the cemetery. I was instantly sorry I'd mentioned it. He didn't need to hear about my life.

"Oh, ya?" He looked at me thoughtfully. "Probably wasn't the best idea to come here, huh?"

"It's okay. It doesn't bother me."

"How long's it been?"

"About a year and a half. I was in seventh grade."

"I would have been in parochial school then. . . . I'm sorry. I didn't know."

"It's okay. Hey, thanks for inviting me for a smoke. And thanks for saying what you did yesterday."

"Huh? Oh, ya. No problem." We didn't say anything for a couple of minutes, just sat looking down over the town. Keith asked, "How did it happen? Car accident?"

"Ya."

"Bummer. . . . Say, you don't have to answer this, but is that why your old man is always so damn grim?"

"Part of it, I guess. Mom was real cheerful and she kept him loose. At least looser than he is now. She worked as a secretary up at the TV station and she always had a lot of funny stories."

"I'll bet. Brandt Mills' claim to fame: the worst TV station east of the Mississippi."

"Probably in the hemisphere, from the way she used to talk. Anyway, she could make Dad laugh. When he was in a bad mood or worried about something, she could get him out of it. Now he always seems to be in a bad mood."

"He sure is strict. Nailed me twice already this year and I keep real clear of him now. None of the other teachers are such hard asses. How come he's always on somebody's case?"

I shrugged. "He says rules are meant to be obeyed, and even if the other teachers don't enforce them, he will."

"I guess I can see his point, but why does he make a big deal out of everything?"

"Damned if I know."

Keith grunted and didn't say anything for a moment. "Well, I guess you get asked that kind of crap all the time. Screw it. Let's talk about something else."

We did, just a relaxed conversation with lots of pauses while we enjoyed the view and the warm sun. When the five-o'clock whistle at the mill blew, I said, "Well, I guess I'd better get home."

"Okay." Keith levered his long frame off the hood. "Hey, I've enjoyed this, man. Let's do it again sometime."

"Sounds good."

Over that winter we became friends. Not real tight, but good, relaxed friends. After the canoe trip in the summer, I figured he'd open up a little more, but he seemed changed when he got back from Milwaukee in the fall. He'd always been quiet, but now he seemed to be distancing himself from everybody—don't touch them and they won't touch me. He'd done his drugs before, but now he started getting really heavy into downers. By second semester he'd stopped going to classes and was spending most of the day sitting in the cafeteria. And even if I was no model student myself, it had really begun to worry me. Still, I didn't want to lose him as a friend by prying too deeply into his personal problems.

In the smoking lounge, I cupped my hand around the Marlboro and got it lit. The snow had stopped, but a cold wind blew through my shirt, chilling me in a moment. Only a half-dozen kids huddled around trying to find a little shelter. Three guys came around the corner giggling. They'd just done a joint and were already feeling the effects. "Hey, Wart," one of them called, "how's it going?"

I shrugged. From long practice I could tell he didn't mean anything nasty by it, just a greeting. When some of the jocks called me Wart, there was a different edge to the word. Not that I liked it either way.

When my cigarette had burned down to the filter, I went back inside, the sudden warmth making me shiver all over again. I went back and sat where I'd left my algebra book. The cover had a bulge and I opened it to find a half-eaten peanut-butter sandwich crushed between the pages. What s.o.b. had done that? I looked over at Keith. "Who?" I choked.

"Vanik." He looked down, absorbed in picking a callus on his palm.

The other guys at the table squirmed in their chairs a little and went on talking quietly. They hated the jocks too, but no one, not even Keith, was going to stand up to Tom Vanik for me.

Behind me the door to the boys' can swung open and I turned to see Vanik come out, a big grin on his face. Walking behind me, he muttered, "How was lunch, Wart?" He rounded the corner and walked down the center aisle between the long cafeteria tables. A burst of laughter and applause from the jock table greeted him and the study-hall supervisors turned to glare. They wouldn't do anything. The jocks could get away with murder. A couple of bitter murmurs rose from my table, but not much. The dirts knew the score. At the far end of the table Perry said something about "that bastard" and Jeff said, "Will you shut up! That mouth of yours is going to get you killed one of these days."

I tried to peel off the crushed sandwich, but the goo stuck to the pages, making oily stains on the paper. My face was burning. I got off what I could and wrapped it in a sheet of notebook paper. I glanced around, then dropped the wad under the table. I wasn't going to the wastebasket and give the jocks any more excuse to laugh.

When the bell rang, I headed for the nearest hall to the classrooms. I wasn't hungry anymore. Besides, it was Dad's day to supervise during lunch and I wanted to avoid seeing him in action. Mr. Wilson, one of the math teachers, stepped sideways into my path. "What did you drop under the table?"

"Nothing."

"Doesn't look like nothing to me. Go pick it up." I wanted to protest, but my excuse was too complicated. I went back.

I had to get down on my hands and knees, and the jocks

sauntered by just as I got hold of the gummy wad. "Looks just like a toad." Vanik snickered. There was laughter.

"Yep," drawled Cummings, "you ought to feed him more often, Tom, so he'll grow up to be just as big a toad as his old man." More laughter. They swaggered over to the lunch line forming next to the stainless-steel counters the cooks had just rolled in.

I was crushing the ball tight in my fist, the goo squirming out between my fingers. Steady, Wart! Stay calm. I took a deep breath, then pulled myself out from under the table. No way was I going to pass by those jerks, so I walked down to the other end of the cafeteria, pitched the ball into the waste-basket, and headed up the far hall, eyes down, watching my shoes scuff the worn floors.

I killed the time until history in a corner of the library, paging through a big picture book on antique cars. If only I had a place to hide, I thought. One of the furnace rooms or something. Just come out for classes and then go back down there to hide. How I had made it this far I couldn't imagine; the rest of the school year stretched like an immeasurable ocean in front of me and I didn't even have a life jacket. Capstone. I just had to get into Capstone.

Mr. Hoffman handed back the papers facedown and I turned mine over to see the big red F and the note, "You will have to do far better to pass the course." Well, that was no news. He went over the test and answered questions, then wrote the assignment on the board and we started reading. The chapter was on the digging of the Panama Canal, not one of my major interests, but I kept dragging myself down the long columns of print until the other kids started gathering up their books. Salvation. Two hours of auto mechanics, the bright spot of my day—of my life, actually.

4

The halls were crowded and noisy—lots of laughter, slamming locker doors, and loud, cheerful talk. The day was winding down. I said "Hi" to three or four guys and a couple of girls I counted as casual friends. By the doors to the home-ec rooms, I saw Trish and called out to her. "Hey, Trish, hold up a sec."

"Oh, hi, Steve." She didn't sound enthusiastic.

"Do you have your algebra assignment?"

"Turned it in last hour, sorry."

Damn, I was going to have to do it myself. A wild thought intercepted my disappointment. I shuffled. "Say, do you want to catch a movie Friday night?" What was I saying? Of course she didn't.

She looked uncomfortable. "I don't know. Well, okay, I guess. Why don't you call me?" She hurried into the room. Hell, she'd just give an excuse on the phone. I walked on toward the shop, wishing I hadn't asked.

My spirits improved on entering the shop. The smell of oil and gasoline enveloped me and I was back in a world I could handle. It's not that I'm great buddies with the guys in the shop or that I avoid all the Wart crap there. Still, almost all the guys are really interested in the work and there isn't much talk or horseplay. Most of the guys are farm kids or working-class kids. There are a couple of dirts, but no jocks or brains. All in all, it's a pretty easygoing bunch, and even when one of them says something like, "Hey, Wart, hand me that socket," I don't mind it much, since I know he probably doesn't know me by any other name. I'm comfortable in the shop—more comfortable than anywhere else.

Mr. Ohm was standing in the middle of the shop in his gray overalls. Somehow they always seem miraculously clean, even after he's been working on a car. He was watching a couple of the guys digging around under the hood of an old Ford. I hurried down to the overall rack, threw my books on top, and started to pull on a pair. Mr. Ohm turned, glanced at the old wristwatch that circled his thick, hairy arm, then looked over at me. I was late. "I'm sorry, Mr. Ohm, I was trying to get an algebra assignment." He nodded, it was all right. Only a minute or two. "I'm finished with that carburetor. Do you have something for me to do?"

"There's a starter over there that needs a new drive. Worked on one before?"

"Couple of times."

"Well, call me when you have it apart."

I found the starter on the far end of the workbench. The label attached read "D. Mattson." Mattson, I thought, I ought to screw this up to get back at the s.o.b. But that was a stupid impulse. I took pride in doing a good job in auto mechanics. I might not be much good at anything else, but nothing and no one was going to mess up the job I did here. I went for some tools.

I knew less about starters than I'd thought, and had to call Mr. Ohm over a couple of times before I had it figured out. He was patient and very deliberate, something that drives a lot of the kids nuts at first. They want to hurry, slap it together fast, and see if it works. But in the end he's twice as efficient.

When cleanup time came, I had the starter half together again, but Mr. Ohm is strict about cleaning up the shop. When he rings the buzzer, you get your parts arranged so you can pick up next time where you left off, and then start putting away tools and sweeping the floor. The time had rushed by and I was surprised when the buzzer sounded. I hadn't thought about Vanik or Cummings or Dad or algebra in almost two hours, and that was pure happiness for me. Capstone—I should talk to Mr. Ohm about that soon.

But reality came back swiftly in homeroom when Mr. Hoffman handed me a note. "Steve, please see me after school, Miss Thomas." What was I going to do now?

I waited outside her office, standing on one foot then the other, while she got done talking to a couple of freshmen basic-math students. When they left, she looked up at me with those pretty brown eyes that were so hard to lie to. "I still need your assignment, Steve."

"I couldn't find it. Must have lost it."

She looked down, pursing her lips. "You failed the quiz too. How could you fail it if you'd done the assignment? It doesn't look like you even started the problem." She held up my quiz with all its silly doodling.

"I didn't understand it very well. I was going to come and ask for some help."

"So you didn't finish the assignment?"

"Well, I kinda got stuck. I tried, though."

She gazed at me for a long five seconds, then looked down again, shaking her head slowly. She flipped the pages of her grade book and followed the line across after my name, her other hand punching numbers on a pocket calculator. She recorded the total. "It doesn't look like you're going to pass this quarter, Steve."

I felt my lungs suck in air sharply. Had I missed that many points? Hell, I'd passed a couple of the tests. Not by much, but passing. "Not even a D−?"

"I'm afraid not. Look here." She ran her finger slowly along the line as I watched. Seven or eight squares had zeros where I'd failed to hand in assignments. Her other hand was totaling the numbers as if it had a life of its own. She didn't even have to look as her thin fingers with their long, carefully kept nails danced on the calculator buttons. The answer came out the same.

42

"If I got those missing assignments in, could I still pass?"

Her eyes were pained; she didn't like this either—not like some of the older teachers who'd flunk a kid at the drop of a pen. "Steve, you know the rules. They've been the same all year. You lose ten points for turning in an assignment at the end of the day and no credit after that."

"Maybe I was sick a couple of those days."

She checked. "No, you were here." She closed the book slowly. "Really, Steve, you've been here long enough to learn the system."

I nodded. She was right.

"Now if you really want to pass the course, you still can. You'll have to do enough of those missing assignments to understand the work coming up, and you'll have to pass the final. If you can do that, you'll get the credit. It's up to you." I nodded again. "Okay?" she asked.

"Ya. Okay." I told her thanks and left. I was numb. Boy, was Dad going to give me hell. How had I gotten so far behind? I couldn't remember.

I'd missed my chance at a ride home with Keith or one of the other guys. I would have walked, but I could see a hard wind blowing snow and wastepaper up against the glass doors at the end of the hall. Outside I'd have to walk the first five blocks straight into that wind. No, better to wait for Dad.

I trudged down to my locker, trying to think of how I was going to tell him about algebra. Better to tell him in advance than to wait for report cards. Still, why bother? Let him get all the bad news at once. At least there was auto mechanics. I'd get a B there for sure, not that Dad would care.

Dad wasn't in his office behind the biology room, so I sat at one of the black lab tables and tried to read some history.

When he came in a half-hour later, I could tell from his face that my day was going to get a whole lot worse. He glared at me, threw a small sheaf of papers on my table, and stomped into his office. I looked down at them in horror. I could hear Dad slamming file drawers open and shut. The papers were handwritten notes from Dad to each of my teachers asking about my progress. Their replies were worse than I could have imagined.

> *Mr. Hoffman, American history: Steve's work on assignments and exams in the last nine weeks has been unsatisfactory. He is poorly prepared and lackadaisical in class. F. He will need a C in the fourth quarter for a passing grade for the year.*

> *Mrs. Rawls, English: Steven is an articulate young man when he chooses to be, but he has put little effort into English all year. Although it pains me, I have to give him a D for the quarter. Sorry.*

> *Mr. Ohm, auto mechanics: Good work. B.*

> *Mr. Lindon, physical education: Steve has average athletic ability, but tends to be lazy and often holds back when a member of a team. C −.*

> *Miss Thomas, algebra: Sorry I didn't get this to you until the end of the day. Your son did not submit seven assignments this quarter and failed most quizzes and two exams. Algebra grades are based on cumulative point totals. Steve earned 346 of 650 points this quarter—390 were required for a D. I have talked with him several times, but he seems to have little but excuses to offer. I hope you can motivate him where I have failed.*

> *Mr. Mattson, Speech I: In a class where a premium is placed on active participation in the preparing, delivering, and critiquing of speeches, your son has failed to exhibit minimum acceptable performance. As the instructor of a half-credit elective, I expect my students to be self-motivated. This is not the case with your son. Providing there is an immediate improvement in attitude, a passing grade can still be attained. However, the chances appear remote at this time, since the student in question seems more concerned with the work in shop class than the necessity of attending and participating in Speech I. I will be happy to talk to you in more detail on this matter. Third-quarter grade: F.*

Dad came out of his office, jerking on his coat. He slammed the door behind him. "Let's go."

I followed him down the hall, my legs wooden under me,

the accusing notes slowly moistening in my palm. I'd blown it; I'd never get into Capstone now. And Dad was going to make my life hell.

The wind hit me like a hammer when I opened the door, but I hardly felt the cold. That heavy north wind was nothing compared to the storm rising behind Dad's set features. I would have given anything, anything in the world, to be going anywhere but home with him. In the car, I sat as far away from him as I could, staring at the dusty door of the glove compartment. The five-o'clock whistle at the mill cried out in the falling darkness.

On Dad's side of the windshield a note flapped hard in the wind, almost tearing loose from under the wiper. Dad got out and pulled it free. Inside, he unfolded it and I glanced over to read it. "Watch out, Toad, or you'll be driving home on the rims!" A half-dozen obscenities followed. Dad's jaw worked as he stared at it, then he crumpled it in his gloved hand, threw it in the back seat, and turned the ignition key viciously. The car roared, or tried to. Boy, did that engine need work. He slammed the Buick in gear and backed out of the parking place, wheels spinning.

The confrontation didn't come right away. Maybe Dad was afraid to open his mouth yet. We got dinner ready in silence. I tried to eat, but the food tasted like cardboard and the TV news on the tabletop portable was just so much background noise. After a second bite of his hamburger, Dad set it carefully on his plate and chewed mechanically. I just sat looking at mine. He took a long drink of coffee and set down the empty cup. "How did it happen, Steven? How in the world could you let this happen?" His voice was tired.

This wasn't what I'd expected. Ranting, shouting, yes. But not this awful fatigue in his voice. All I could do was shrug and mumble, "I don't know. I didn't think it was this bad."

"Well, it's pretty bad, isn't it?" He shook his head. "I don't know what your mother would say if she could see us now."

I cringed. That was a low blow and I could feel it all the

way through me. Why now? Couldn't we leave her out of it after all these years?

He sighed and got up to get water for more coffee. A long pause followed as he measured a teaspoon of instant, poured hot water into the cup, and sat stirring it slowly, his eyes gazing at the black eddy of the liquid. He tapped the spoon on the rim of the cup and took a swallow. "Well, I've decided to give you every chance to pass. From now on, no TV, no allowance, no going out, and no screwing around. Every night after the dishes, you'll go to your room and study. If you make it, fine. If you don't, no one can say I didn't do my level best." He paused, took a deep breath, and looked up at me, his face pale but firm. "I'm tired of it, Steven. Just sick-to-death tired of it. For the past three years I've done everything I could to be both parents to you, but you refuse to cooperate. I'd hoped you'd grow out of it, but you don't seem to care what you make of yourself."

He looked down, slowly stiring the coffee again. A bitter resentment almost came to my tongue. Don't blame me if you're a lousy parent, Toad. I've done my best. But instead of saying anything, I got up and walked to my room, a lump the size of an egg in my throat. Ya, done my best. That was a lot of crap too. For maybe half an hour I sat at my desk with my head in my hands, staring out through my fingers at my un-opened books. I could hear Dad putting away food and dishes, then sitting down in front of the TV to correct papers. At least he wasn't coming in.

Finally, I sat back and tried to think. What was I going to do? I couldn't stand two more years of school without Capstone. Hell, I wasn't sure I could stand the nine weeks left in this year. Was there still a chance of getting into Capstone? I had to be kidding. I'd blown it but good. So, what then? I was sixteen, and if Dad signed for me, I could drop out and get a job. But he'd never do it. Not now anyway. Maybe I should just sit out the year and then tell him I wasn't going back no matter what he said. If he wouldn't sign, I'd move out.

But even as I considered that, some semblance of pride deep

in me argued against it. Damn it, I had to make it! If I could just get into Capstone I could survive the last two years and walk out of school with my head up despite all they'd been able to do to me. And I'd just keep walking—out of Brandt Mills High, out of Brandt Mills, out of the life I'd lived. I wasn't going to be flunked out of it.

I took a sheet of paper and calculated my grade point average. Was it still possible to get a C average? After all, I'd done better the first two quarters. Yes, it was still possible. Just barely. Boy, would I have to work. I got out my English. Simplest things first.

About nine o'clock I walked into the kitchen to call Trish. I'd gotten through the English by then and had tried to read a little more history. Failing in that, I'd started looking back through my algebra text to pick up the missing thread of the work. But the seemingly endless pages of formulas and problems left me discouraged. It seemed impossible to get a handle on it. A month must have passed since I'd had the foggiest idea of what was going on.

Trish answered on the third ring. Good, at least I wouldn't have to talk to anyone else. She had a brother who was a freshman and I could almost hear him yelling, "Hey, Trish. The Wart is on the phone."

"Hi, Trish, this is Steve."

"Hi, Steve."

She didn't sound very happy to hear me, but it didn't make any difference now. I plunged ahead before she could say any more. "About Friday night, my old man and I had a blowup and I'm grounded."

"Oh. That's too bad." Did I hear relief in her voice? "Nothing too awful, I hope."

"Well, it's not too good. He's pretty upset about my grades."

"Algebra?"

"Ya, that and a couple of others. Say, do you suppose I could see your assignment in the morning?"

"It isn't due until Friday, so I might not have it done."

"Well, when you have it finished."

"Okay, but, you know, it's not going to help you pass the tests much if you're just copying from me."

"Ya, I know, but I need some help until I can get caught up."

"Well, okay. Sorry you got grounded."

"Ya, thanks. Maybe some other time."

"Sure."

Sure, I'll bet, I thought as I hung up the phone and went to see what was in the refrigerator. She's as pleased as anything to get out of it. Well, I just won't ask her again. I'm going to be locked up here until summertime anyway.

5

Thursday the teachers had their end-of-quarter faculty meeting, so school was dismissed at one o'clock, leaving me with a few hours of freedom before Dad got home. Keith had an appointment with Mattson, so I waited for him in the hall outside the administration office. About one-fifteen he came out and I could tell from his tense face that things hadn't gone well. "What did he say?" I asked.

"Tell you about it in the car." He pulled on his stocking cap and zipped his coat. His fingers shook slightly. Mattson had really gotten to him; Keith almost never lets any emotion show.

Walking through the faculty lot to where the students park, we passed Dad's Buick. Another note was stuck under a wiper. I hesitated, then took the note and shoved it in my pocket.

A block from school in Keith's rusted Impala, he asked, "What's the note?"

I was almost afraid to look, but I did. "It says, 'You didn't get the message, Toad. Back off or we'll tear this car apart. You . . .' And there are a bunch of cuss words."

"Jocks," Keith said. "Your old man laid into Cummings, Vanik, and their crowd again today."

"Oh, God, what about this time?"

Keith shrugged. "Don't know. Something about hall passes, I think."

I groaned. "Damn. Why can't he lay off?"

"He should. Those guys might just do what they say."

We were driving through the outskirts of town. The car was warming up now. Keith took off his cap and shook out his shoulder-length hair.

"You got bad trouble with Mattson?" I asked.

He grimaced. "You sure got that one right. He said if I didn't start going to classes, he was going to have me expelled."

"Can he do that?"

"I guess. He showed me some of the stuff in my file. Looks like they've got the paperwork done already."

"I bet he was just trying to scare you."

"Maybe, but I don't think so this time. Screw 'em. Let's talk about something else."

We talked about music for a while, but my thoughts kept returning to school. Could I still make it? Was it worth the effort, or should I just sit out the year and see what the summer brought?

"What are you going to do, Keith? I mean, about Mattson and all?"

"Don't know. I can't pass much even if I start going to classes. Maybe I'll drop out."

"Will your parents sign for you?"

"Hard to tell. Depends how sober they are." He laughed his bitter, humorless laugh. "And how much they want to get rid of me this week."

"My dad would never consider it. Hell, he still thinks I'll eventually go to college."

"You still got a chance for that Capstone thing?"

"Not much."

We rode in silence for ten minutes, listening to the radio and our private thoughts. Keith drove in a wide circle around the south of town, following country roads flanked by prosperous farms.

"Maybe I'll work on a farm this summer," I said—the thought had never occurred to me before.

Keith glanced at me curiously, then laughed softly. "Boy, things really must be tough at home. You're not exactly the farming type."

"Ya, I guess you're right. I'd just like to get away from Dad for a while. I don't care where or what I'd have to do."

"I know the feeling."

For a second I felt guilty about complaining about my life. Keith had it even rougher. I changed the subject. "Hey, you got any grass?"

"Wish I did. There ain't been much around the last few days. Maybe tomorrow. You want a red?"

I was tempted, but I don't get along very well with downers. "No, I'd better not. Thanks anyway."

"Sure."

"Say, are you still seeing that social worker about that thing in the fall?"

"Not very often. I think she's given up on me." He laughed. "We got off pretty lucky on that one."

"Ya, it could have been a lot worse."

God knows it had been bad enough.

Back in October the four of us were riding around in Keith's car late on a beautiful afternoon. It was Friday, time to relax. We'd smoked a couple of joints and were feeling pretty mellow, humming along with the radio and enjoying the scenery. Fall is the best time in Wisconsin. The air is crisp, the insects are gone, and the woods burst with color. Autumn doesn't last long, less than a month, but it's some compensation for the long winter ahead.

It would have been nice to have some girls along, but it was okay with just the four of us, too. There aren't many dirt girls, but they make up for it by being pretty rowdy, and we weren't in that kind of mood. Jeff, riding in the back seat with Perry, had just suggested we start planning a canoe trip for the spring when Keith yelped, "Holy shit, there's a cop behind us!" I looked back in terror. A dark-maroon county cop car was a half-dozen car lengths behind with its red lights flashing. "Hide everything!" Keith said, grabbing the bag of grass and shoving it into what he calls his stash, a long narrow crack in the middle of the front seat. The bag made only the faintest bulge in the worn plastic. "Open your window, Steve. It must smell like hell in here."

We slowed to a stop and sat waiting as the cop, a chunky, middle-aged guy, got out of his car and came to Keith's window. "May I see your driver's license, sir?"

"Sure. What's the matter, Officer?"

"Your left brake light isn't working." He studied Keith's license and then looked over at me. "Why do you have your window open, son?"

"Me?" I said.

"Yes, you."

"I don't know. Fresh air, I guess."

He held me with a long, hard stare for what seemed like a minute, then turned on his heel and walked back to his car.

Perry leaned forward, his voice hoarse with fear. "He's on to us, Freakman. Throw the grass out Steve's window."

"Can't. He's watching us." Keith had his eyes turned to the rearview mirror.

"What are we going to do?" Perry was close to panic. I felt like heaving I was so scared.

"Put the stuff behind the back seat. He'll never look there." Jeff was whispering for no reason.

"Hey, don't put it back near me," Perry said.

"Shut up," Keith snapped. "It's too late anyway. Now don't hype out, guys. He probably just called to check for tickets on the car."

The cop came back to Keith's window. "Okay, boys, I have reason to believe you were smoking marijuana. Now, do you want to tell me about it or do I search the car?"

"We weren't doin' nothin'," Keith protested.

The cop snorted. "Come on, your car reeks of it." No one said anything. "Well, you think about it until my backup gets here." He straightened.

The next five minutes were some of the longest in my life. I imagine the others felt the same as we fidgeted, too afraid even to whisper. Another cop car cleared the hill a half-mile ahead and came down the hard-packed gravel road, leaving only a slender trail of dust to blow across the fields. He slowed and swung over to our side of the road and stopped, cutting off our line of escape as if we'd been big-time criminals. A tall, younger cop with a mustache got out. "What's up, Frank?"

"Got a car needs searching." Frank looked in at us. "Anybody want to talk, now?" No one said anything. The cop sighed, sounding tired and a little bored. "Okay, boys, get out of the car. Stand by the front and be quiet."

We got out and stood nervously in a knot. The younger cop looked us up and down, decided we were no immediate danger, and stepped closer to Keith's car so he could watch the search. The older cop started with the back seat, then after five minutes moved on to the front. Another five minutes passed as he dug around. Could he possibly miss it? It seemed so obvious. I glanced at Keith, who was looking on impassively, arms folded. I turned back to watch the cops, trying not to look guilty or hopeful. I could hear Perry and Jeff shuffling and whispering behind us. "Can they search us?" "I don't know. I suppose so. You hot?" "I've got some papers, that's all. Is that a crime?" "Don't be stupid. We'd better be quiet."

"Here it is." The older cop stood up holding the bag. Behind me Jeff groaned softly and Perry said, "Damn." Keith didn't even twitch, but the back of my legs started to shake and I was afraid I was going to vomit. The cop turned to us. "Well, boys, I'm going to have to take you in for questioning. Procedure says we search you first. You might as well tell me now if you have any drugs . . . or weapons." The other cop smirked at that and the older one glanced coldly at him. "Chuck, you might as well read them their rights. Okay"—he pointed at me—"you first."

I couldn't believe it. I'd walked into a bad TV movie, or maybe this was a nightmare. I leaned against the car and he patted me down. "Okay, put your hands behind your back."

My God, he was going to cuff me! I felt the cool metal around my wrists. In the background, a million miles away, I could hear the young cop reading the rights. I must have shown how scared I felt, because the older cop gave me an almost friendly slap on the shoulder. "Stand over by the trunk." Suddenly my nose gushed blood. "Oh, hell," he said. "Lean forward." I did and the blood fell on the road instead of the front of my shirt.

The others were watching. "Probably sue you for police brutality, Frank," the young cop said with a laugh.

The older cop growled, "Oh, shut up." He undid the cuffs and the young cop, still chuckling, went back to reading the rights. My hands free, I pulled out my handkerchief and crushed it to my nose. I was so embarrassed I felt like crying. "You going to be okay?" I nodded. "All right, raise your other hand." He refastened the cuffs in front of me. "Okay?" I nodded again and he turned away to search Jeff. The young cop finished reading the rights and gave Perry and Keith a perfunctory search. They didn't cuff Keith.

Finished, the older cop said, "Chuck, you take one and I'll take the other two. Mr. Miller, you drive between us. Understand?" Keith nodded. "Okay, let's go."

Jeff went with the young cop, and Perry and I walked awkwardly to the other squad car. The cop helped me into the back seat and slammed the door. As he helped Perry in the other side, I tried to comprehend what was happening to us. But it was too huge, too incredible. My God, we'd only been smoking grass. Everyone did it. Or almost everyone. But now we were on the way to the police station in a squad car with our hands cuffed. It was absurd! What were they going to do to us? Worse yet, what was Dad going to do to me?

A couple of miles down the road, Perry asked in a weak voice, "Uh, what happens now?"

"That'll depend."

For a second I thought Perry was going to ask, "Depend on what?" But he must have been too scared of the answer, all his usual hotheaded courage squelched by the enormity of it all.

We rode the rest of the way in silence behind Keith's car.

By the time we got to town my nose had stopped bleeding, but my hands and face were sticky with drying blood.

Brandt Mills is the county seat and the sheriff's department is in the courthouse, a grim, cold building, stained dark by the smoke from the mill. Inside the station the older cop took off our cuffs, collected our drivers' licenses, asked our phone numbers, and then went behind the desk to call our parents.

Perry started to whisper something to Jeff, but a female deputy looking in one of the file cabinets shook her finger at him and we all sat silent. After a minute she said to me, "There's a bathroom over by the pop machine. Go ahead and use it. Be quick."

I hurried in and washed my face in cold water. At least they allowed you to have a clean face. I was grateful for that—a shred of dignity before the firing squad lined up.

When I came back in, the older cop had just gotten Dad on the phone. "Hello, Mr. Michaels? . . . This is Deputy Sheriff Olson. . . . No, no accident. We have your son and three other boys in custody for suspected use of marijuana. . . . That's correct. He was riding in a vehicle where marijuana was being smoked. . . . Yes, of course. . . . All right, I'll wait until you arrive."

He said pretty much the same thing to the other parents, although he had to repeat himself a couple of times when talking to Keith's mother. Then he led Keith through a door marked Interrogation Room, and the three of us sat in the watchful care of the female deputy.

About ten minutes later Dad came hurrying through the door. He saw me immediately and came over. I avoided his eyes. "Steven, what is going on?" I shrugged. "That's not an answer. Look at me!" I looked. "Did you smoke marijuana?" I looked down again. "Ya, I tried a puff or two." He stood for a half-minute leaning over me, then gave an infinitely tired sigh and went to a chair on the other side of the room and sat brooding.

About five minutes later the cop and Keith came out of the

room. I watched Keith for some sign. He nodded his head slightly. So, he'd admitted it.

Dad was standing. "Deputy Olson?"

"Yes, you are. . . ?"

"John Michaels."

"Glad to meet you, sir." They shook hands. "I'm going to question your son next. You have the right to be present, but we usually find these things go better if the parent waits out here." Dad hesitated, then nodded. "Steven, this way please."

I got up and walked ahead of the cop to the room—again not looking at Dad. Inside, the cop pointed to a chair, then sat down on the other side of a big table. "Do you know what the Miranda warning is, Steven?" I nodded. "Well, listen carefully anyway." He read the rights familiar to anybody who watches TV cop shows: you have the right to this, the right to that, etc. "Do you understand your rights, Steven?" I nodded. "Sign here." He indicated a place on a form and I signed a shaky signature. He asked some routine questions about age and so forth, entering the answers on the form, then got down to business. "Was marijuana smoked in the car?" I nodded. "Did you smoke some?" I nodded. "Whose was it?"

"Keith's."

"Did anyone else bring some?"

"I don't know. I don't think so."

"Where did he buy it?"

"I don't know."

And so it went. He asked me lots of things, like when I'd first smoked grass, how often did I smoke, where did I get it, and who were the big dealers in school. I was vague in my answers. We'd been caught, but I wasn't going to turn narc. After ten minutes of rephrasing and repeating the questions, he gave up and took me back out. Dad got up. "Mr. Michaels, we'll have a brief statement for your son to sign in a few minutes, then you can take him home. I'm issuing him a county citation for use of marijuana. Jeffrey, step this way."

He led Jeff away and we sat down. Perry's mother had arrived and sat teary-eyed by Perry, who was hunched up in

56

his coat, staring at the floor. Keith was standing by the pop machine smoking a cigarette. We exchanged glances.

Fifteen minutes later I signed the statement, picked up the citation, and followed Dad out to the car. I was surprised to read on the ticket that the fine was only twenty-five dollars. They make a pretty big deal out of it for twenty-five lousy bucks, I thought.

Dad didn't talk all the way home, but when I turned from hanging up my coat, he was standing only a foot away from me. His voice was almost a hiss. "Don't you ever do that again! You may not give a damn about your reputation, but mine means something to me."

"Dad—"

"Shut up! I don't want you to see those kids anymore, and if you ever smoke that crap again, I will beat the living shit out of you."

I was stunned. Dad had never said anything like that before. We stared at each other for a long minute, then he turned angrily away and marched into the living room, where he stood looking at the picture of Mom and Roxy on the corner table.

Keith had a black eye when he came to school the next Monday.

We came back into town from the east. Keith drove slowly up the long main street. On this March afternoon the town looked dreary and sad. "You wanta get a Coke?" he asked.

"Okay. Wish we had some beer."

"You really need something today, huh? How about that red?"

"No, I don't like those much."

"Well, you're probably lucky. They ain't much good for you." We turned in at Mac's, got Cokes from the drive-up window, then sat in the car drinking them. "What are you going to do about the note that was on your dad's windshield?"

"Throw it away, I guess. It would only upset him and I don't want to have to listen to him."

"It must be tough being the only one around to catch the crap at your house. At least I've got brothers and sisters— shitscreens, that's what I call them."

I laughed. Shitscreens. I'd have to remember that one. "Ya, I could use a couple of those. I get pelted pretty regular."

"Do you think your dad will ever get remarried?"

"Who'd have him? Or what?" We laughed—it did bring images. Marry Dad to a grizzly or something. "I don't know. Someday, maybe. He isn't looking. I think he still misses Mom a lot."

"Don't you?"

"Sometimes, but . . . well, it's been a long time."

Keith grunted. I felt him slipping away. He does that a lot. You can be talking to him and then suddenly he isn't listening anymore, lost in his own distant, bitter thoughts. Maybe it's the downers, or maybe something else. I don't know, but it worries me.

6

Dad hadn't been kidding about my grounding rules. Thursday night I was banished to my room to study, although I didn't do much except page disconsolately through the algebra book, trying a simple problem here and there.

Friday was uneventful. Classes went okay—no quizzes and no questions directed my way. I got Mattson's starter back together during auto mechanics, but it still didn't work right, so I tore it down and started over. I managed to avoid Dad, Cummings, and Vanik all day. So, everything considered, it was a good day.

I caught a ride with Keith after school, but he was even less talkative than usual. I'd hoped we could do a joint, but he still didn't have any grass. "Well," I said, "maybe we could drive out to that country place where they let you buy beer. I've got money for a six-pack and we've got a couple of hours before I've got to be home."

He looked at me for a moment, then said, "No, I'm sorry, man. I've got a couple of things I've gotta do . . . kind of private things."

I was disappointed. Hell, I wouldn't be able to go out all weekend and Keith was going to dump me off at home during the little time I had free.

He seemed to realize that I was a little hurt. When I got out, he said gently, "Hey, be cool, man. We'll see you."

Friday evening, while everyone else was out having a good

time, I sat at my desk and studied. Or at least tried to. But even with Capstone riding on my grades, I couldn't concentrate. Hell, I'd worked all week—or at least survived. For the Wart, that was work enough. Why should I have to stay in on a Friday night? A few hours out would make me better able to study later. That sounded reasonable, but I didn't even try it on Dad.

The only break on Saturday was a chance to do the weekly shopping with Dad. Normally I hate it and try to make excuses to get out of going. I don't want to be seen with Dad anywhere, even the grocery store. But this Saturday I was so crazy to escape the apartment I looked forward to it all morning.

Sunday morning we went to church. We almost always do. Sometimes we'll miss in the summer, but otherwise, it's just like when Mom and Roxy were alive. Then we'd all stand together in a pew near the front. Mom would poke me every once in a while to keep me singing during the hymns or to make me sit up straight during the sermon. I was bored with church even then, but now I remember those Sundays as golden. After Sunday school, we'd ride around town a little or drive out into the country if it was a nice day. Sunday dinner was always special, even if we didn't have guests, and I remember how we'd talk and laugh and have fun around the table. I suppose there were a lot of Sundays when Roxy and I were whiny and Dad and Mom irritable, but I don't remember those times much. I just think back to when I had a real family and lived in a real house with a real front yard and . . . and what? Felt like I was really loved? To hell with it. That was a long time ago.

Dad only goes up for communion Christmas and Easter. Back when Mom and Roxy were alive, he went up every Sunday, but not since the accident. I asked him about it a couple of times, but he just shook his head and didn't answer. Maybe he denies himself for some reason, or maybe he just doesn't believe like he used to. I go up every Sunday, even

60

though I can't say I really believe very much, but he'd squawk if I didn't and, well, I want to believe.

This Sunday Trish was in the other line a couple of paces ahead of me. When I got to the rail, I glanced over to where she knelt, head bowed, eyes closed. She looked good in a green dress with her long brown hair falling over her shoulders. Not beautiful, but gentle and good. I turned away and concentrated on the ceremony. Letting my thoughts about Trish run on wasn't exactly in keeping with church.

When I passed by her pew on the way back to my seat, she smiled and I smiled back. Lord, how she did fill out the top of that dress! I almost wished I was going to Sunday school so I could watch her and maybe talk to her a little, but attending Sunday school was one argument I'd won with Dad. A year before, when the class got a particularly stupid guy for a teacher, I'd told Dad I'd had it and wouldn't go anymore. It took some hard convincing, but he finally agreed, in part because I think he wanted an excuse to skip the coffee-and-doughnut hour the adults have in the church hall after service. Now it would be a little difficult to tell him why I wanted to go to Sunday school.

Sunday evening after supper, I lay on my bed reading a hot-rod magazine. Hell, I'd worked almost all weekend. Sure, I'd wasted some time staring into space or fiddling with other things, but I'd gotten through more homework than I had in weeks. Now I needed a rest. At least next week would be short with Thursday and Friday off for teachers' convention. Dad never went, so he'd have to report to school and I'd have those two days to take it easy. Maybe I'd even invite some of the guys over. If we were careful, he'd never know. Or maybe I'd invite Trish over to "work" on algebra. Ha, there was a fantasy. Dream on, Wart.

But something gnawed at me. I'd forgotten something. What the hell was it? Damn! That lousy demonstration speech! I was sure to be one of the first ones called on after pissing off Mattson by skipping class on Tuesday. What the hell was I going to talk about? I jumped off the bed and looked around my room wildly. Demonstrate? About all I could demonstrate was how to flunk algebra. My gaze fell on the brick I use to prop up the broken leg on my bed. Demonstrate a brick? Why not? No moving parts anyway.

I tore a sheet of paper out of a notebook and sat down at my desk to make some notes. Let's see. A paperweight, that's a good one. A nutcracker, there's another. Doorstop. Couple more. Minute apiece. Pencil sharpener. Weird, but it would get a laugh. Barbell. Five uses, five minutes. I felt clever and a lot better. I made a rough outline and recopied it carefully, trying to spell everything right.

In the morning I had the brick on top of my school books when we walked out to the car. Dad looked at it speculatively. "What do you need that for?"

"I'm using it in a speech."

"Mattson's class, huh? Figures he'd have you doing something stupid." Dad was just letting his dislike of Mattson show, but he was probably right about the stupid part. The more I'd thought about my speech, the stupider the idea had sounded. Still, I couldn't think of anything better, so I tried to reassure myself. After all, I only needed to pass.

My classes that morning weren't too bad and I began to think I'd survive the day. In gym we went to the pool. I can swim pretty well and I hoped Lindon noticed. C — because I wasn't a team player. What a lot of bull. I'd like to see him be a team player with the other kids always calling him Wart. But I didn't care what he thought; at least I wouldn't fail gym.

We had a quiz in history, but I'd read enough of the chapter to get a C. It didn't count for much, but it was at least a start on the fourth quarter. Speech class met last hour, so I had study hall before to get my thoughts together. I wanted to talk to Keith about my speech, but his tall figure wasn't occupying the usual place. I said "Hi" to Perry and a couple of the other guys and sat by myself at the end of the table. I was nervous as hell, but I kept telling myself I only had to pass, not get an A or something.

I was trying to calm down, repeating that to myself, when Fred came up. He's a big, powerful kid with a brown, pockmarked face and straight black hair like an Indian. "Hey, Wart, your dad get any interesting mail recently?"

I was taken aback. I didn't want to be any part of this. Hell, couldn't they see I didn't get along with him either? "What do you mean?" I couldn't think of anything else to say.

His eyes turned hot. "You know. Notes."

I looked down, my hands nervously shredding the corner of my outline. "Ya. There were a couple on the windshield last week. He didn't show them to me."

"He didn't say anything?"

I shook my head. "No, he was too busy laying crap on me about my grades."

"Oh, ya? What classes?"

I looked up at his face for a hint of understanding. "History, algebra, speech. Doing pretty lousy in all of them."

"So, you gonna be a junior next year?"

"Maybe."

He laughed harshly. Damn! I shouldn't have told him. "Well, that would really piss the old Toad off if his precious Wart got held back." He smirked and strolled away with that arrogant jock swagger.

At the far table I could see Vanik and Cummings watching expectantly amid their group of willing henchmen. What had I done, for God's sake? Tried to get a little sympathy and now they knew enough to ride me down like wolves on a tired deer. Stupid! How incredibly stupid! I watched numbly as Fred told them and they rocked back with laughter, ignoring the supervisor across the room, who glared and gestured at them to be quiet.

Blood spattered on my outline and I grabbed my bleeding nose. It had been months since this had happened! I dug for a handkerchief, trying to catch the blood in my other hand. I didn't even have a piece of tissue, so I rushed for the

63

bathroom, leaving a trail of red spots on the floor. I knew half the study hall would be watching, and that made the blood gush even harder, squirting through my fingers and onto the front of my shirt.

Inside, I was holding a wet paper towel to my nose and trying to hack the blood out of my throat when the door swung open. If it was Fred, Cummings, Vanik, or one of the others, I would vomit. I swallowed hard and started choking on the blood. I felt a big hand on my shoulder.

"You okay?" It was Mr. Lindon, my gym teacher.

I coughed up blood and spat. "Ya, I'm okay."

"Let me see." I leaned back and he looked. Taking the bridge of my nose between fore and middle fingers, he pinched hard. It hurt. "Hold on." He wiped blood from my lip with a towel. "Seems to be pretty well stopped." He kept pinching my nose for another minute as I stood breathing through my mouth. My watering eyes were almost covered by his fingers, but when I heard the door open again, I looked past his big knuckles to see a couple of the jocks come in and stand leaning into the urinals, glancing our way now and then. They left.

"This happen often?" Mr. Lindon asked, taking his hand away.

"Every once in a while."

"Hmmm. Well, maybe you'd better go up to the office and lie down for a few minutes."

"Can't. I've got a speech to give."

"Well, you know best, but take it easy." He slapped me on the arm and left. I washed my face, feeling both embarrassed and thankful. He hadn't had to help. He was a pretty good guy. I'd have to try a little harder in gym.

The bell had rung several minutes before and the crowd in the halls was already thinning when I made it to my locker and grabbed the brick. Trying not to run, I hurried down the hall to Mattson's room. The door was already closed. I took a deep breath and ducked in. Lorie Walker stood behind the tabletop podium about to start her speech. Mattson stared coldly at me from his seat in the back of the class as I slid into my desk. I should have asked Lindon for a note. Now I already had a strike against me. I sat upright and attentive, as if this was something I'd been looking forward to.

Lorie demonstrated how to make paper flowers from tissue paper, her hands quick and sure with the scissors, her voice clear and confident. Finished, she handed in her outline and waited at the front as the class made out critique sheets. Mattson asked for comments. They were all good. These oral critiques could be brutal; Mattson didn't take poor preparation lightly, but so far class was going well.

Jeff, my only close friend in the class, followed Lorie. I'd been foolish enough to let him talk me into taking speech in the first place. I'd figured it would be pretty simple to get a C, since Jeff keeps up on his homework and would let me copy. But now he was getting a B and I was flunking. So much for another bright plan of the Wart's.

Jeff showed how to sharpen a knife and got good comments. Hal Skrypinski came next and talked about how to choose the right length cross-country skis. His speech ran a little long and one of the other guys took issue with a couple of the things he said, but he got off pretty well too. Between the speeches, I tried to smooth out the shredded edge of my outline and scrape the spots of blood off with a fingernail. I was beginning to think maybe I wouldn't have to speak today, but as soon as Hal sat down, Mattson called on me. "Mr. Michaels, are you ready?"

I nodded, took the brick, and got from my desk to the podium despite my shaking legs. I'd forgotten my outline at my desk and had to go back for it. There was a giggle or two. Finally, I stood behind the table with my hands resting on either side of the podium. The outline swam before my eyes. I was intensely conscious of seconds passing and forced myself to take a deep breath. I tried to smile. Here goes. Try to make them laugh a little—the best defense.

"This, ladies and gentlemen, is a brick." I thumped it down on the table. "A brick has many interesting and productive

65

functions. We can use bricks for building walls and barbecue pits, but we often forget many less obvious uses. For example, a brick can be used as a paperweight." I had no paper. I fumbled for my outline and put it under the brick. "See, no matter how hard the wind blows, the paper can't possibly come free." I tugged at the outline and a large corner tore off. The class laughed and I felt my face begin to flush. My nose was going to start bleeding for sure. I hesitated. What came next? I pulled my outline free and checked frantically.

"Another use is as a doorstop." I rushed to the door, tore it open, and put the brick on the floor by it. "See." I was leaning over, half-turned toward the class like some spastic stork—more giggles. They were laughing in the wrong places and I could see Mattson, tight-lipped, mark something on his critique sheet.

I scooped up the brick and tried to walk calmly back to the podium, raising the brick up over my head, then out at arm's length. "And then it can also be used as a barbell or a Polish bowling ball." I slipped my fingers in the holes and made a motion like throwing a bowling ball. It had popped out, a dumb joke. Mattson's face came up hard and dangerous as the class laughed. Jeff shook his head and looked down.

"And also"—I was dead, I knew it, but I lurched on—"it can be used as a nutcracker." I fumbled in my pocket for the walnut I'd been carrying all day. This was wrong. This was supposed to be the finale, the big laugh line. I dropped the nut on the table and brought the brick down like a hinge, almost crushing my own fingers and giving the walnut a glancing blow that sent it skittering off the table and across the floor. Hal caught it and flipped it back to me. The class was howling with laughter. I dealt the walnut a savage blow, showering the table with broken shells and nutmeats.

What was the last one? I grabbed my outline. Somehow I had to finish. Pencil sharpener, the screwiest one. "And, finally, you can use your brick as a pencil sharpener." I ripped a pencil out of my pocket and rapidly rubbed the side of the lead on the rough top of the brick. The pencil snapped with an audible crack. I stood helplessly with the two pieces in my hand and the laughter thundering down on me. In less than five minutes I'd destroyed what little dignity remained to me.

Mattson cleared his throat and slowly the laughter ebbed. "Well, Mr. Michaels, a most interesting speech. May I have your outline?" I took it to him, complete with shredded edge, torn corner, and bloodstains. He frowned down at it as I returned to the front. Kids whispered and giggled as I waited. Jeff and one or two others were looking away in embarrassment. "Well, class"—Mattson drew his hands together in a peak—"I think we have just received a demonstration of how not to make a demonstration speech. A good presentation begins, like everything else in speech, with organization and practice. It would appear that our colleague has done little of either. Now the idea had some merit, but haphazard preparation nullified any possibility of success. Add a tasteless ethnic joke to the speaker's lack of poise, coming undoubtedly from his disorganized preparation, and we have the perfect formula for disaster. Unless you have some defense, Mr. Michaels, you may sit down and we'll get on about business."

The class was hushed now, no more giggling or snide comments. It's uncomfortable to watch even a Wart burned at the stake. I stood looking into Mattson's cold, unfeeling face, and suddenly all my hatred roared to the surface. My hand shot out and grabbed the brick. For a millisecond I thought of heaving it at those hard, vindictive eyes. Instead, I hurled it down on the table, gouging a long slash across the Formica. The brick leaped six feet into the room, bounced once on the floor, and crashed into the wall, fragments breaking away to ricochet across the tiles. I could hear myself screaming. "To hell with your goddamn class! I worked just as hard as anyone else. It made just as much sense as cutting out paper flowers."

"Mr. Michaels, control yourself!" Mattson was standing, anger mixed with alarm on his face.

"And to hell with you and all your picky, cruel comments!" I was pointing at him, my finger shaking. "If you think I'm going to stay here and take your crap anymore, you're dumber than I thought."

I charged out the door and half-ran, half-stumbled toward the nearest exit. Twenty feet down the hall, I heard Mattson's voice raging after me. "You're right about that, Mr. Michaels, you are not going to stay in my class anymore. Go to my office immediately."

"Screw you," I yelled, my voice almost a sob.

I hit the rarely used opposite door and stumbled over a snowbank to the walk leading from the administration wing to the street. I had no coat, but I didn't care about the cold. I didn't try to stop crying either—the snot from my nose mixing with bloody mucus, then fresh blood, as the tears ran down my face.

7

I needed somewhere to go, someplace to hide—any place but home. I walked with my head down toward the poorer section of town, where the houses huddle in the shadow of the big paper mill. I stayed off the main streets, terrified of the curious glances of passing motorists. The blowing snow stung my exposed skin and the wind tore through my thin shirt like the teeth of a saw.

A block from Keith's house, I paused long enough to scrub my face with snow from a dirty pile. The icy crystals burned my hands and gouged my cheeks, but the desire for a clean face, a sliver of dignity, made me scrub all the harder. Gasping with pain, I used my shirttail to rub away what I could of the snot, blood, and tears, then shoved the wet, freezing cloth back into my pants.

At the back of his house I mounted the stairs next to three overflowing garbage cans. My numbed fingers barely felt the paint-flaked surface of the door as I knocked. I waited for what seemed an hour, then knocked again. Finally, a little blond girl about three, dressed in a grimy T-shirt and ragged slacks, hauled the door inward. She stood looking at me with wide brown eyes.

"Is Keith home?"

She shook her head.

"Who is it, Jana?" The woman's voice was nasty. The little girl ran off, leaving me alone on the step staring into the

69

cluttered back porch. A big woman with huge breasts sagging low inside a torn sweatshirt came onto the porch. An infant in diapers hung in the crook of her meaty right arm. "Ya, what is it?"

"I'm looking for Keith."

"I ain't seen him. Ain't seen him since Saturday morning."

"Do you know where he's gone?"

"No, and I don't much care either. He left some kinda note about going to see friends. You seen him?" Her pig-eyes were suspicious.

"No."

"Well, if you do, you tell him his boss called and he's fired and his pa is going to beat the hell out of him when he gets back and finds out." I didn't say anything. "You tell him, hear." Her words reeked of liquor.

"Okay."

"And you tell him that as far as I'm concerned he can just stay away this time. No-good, worthless punk."

I stood looking at her, my chin quivering with cold and disappointment. Finally, I muttered "thanks" and turned away, hearing the door slam and the glass rattle in the loose frame.

I needed a place to hide, but there was nowhere. I wondered if Keith's mother had noticed I'd been crying. Maybe it didn't show anymore. No, it would.

The walk back across town was even worse. I shivered violently every step of the way. Still, I took the long way down alleys and back streets to avoid any of the kids or teachers driving home from school. The prospect of meeting Dad at home was so dreadful I couldn't even think about it. If it hadn't been for the cold, I wouldn't have gone home at all. Just kept on walking.

His car wasn't parked in front of the building and no lights shone in the windows of our apartment. The five-o'clock whistle at the mill had blown when I was three blocks away from the apartment, so Dad was already late.

I let myself in and walked to my bedroom. I stripped off my

frigid clothes, curled myself in a blanket, and waited with the lights off. I drowsed and came awake with a start when I heard the outside door open. The clock next to my bed said six-twenty. Dad came to my door and stood there a moment, then turned and walked back to the kitchen. "He's in there on the bed."

"Does he look okay?" It was Mr. Ohm's voice.

"I think so. I'll call you later. Thanks, Fritz. I appreciate your help."

"He's a good boy, John. Don't be too rough on him."

At that I started crying again.

"Sure. I'll call you. Thanks again."

I heard the door close and I wiped away the tears with a corner of the blanket.

Dad came in and sat on my chair, looking down at his clenched hands. Three or four minutes edged away on the clock before he spoke. "Why'd you do it?"

"I don't know." My voice was little more than a whisper.

There was a long pause. Dad pushed up his glasses and rubbed his eyes. Fatigue? Tears? I couldn't tell. "Where were you?"

"I walked over to a friend's. He wasn't home."

"I was worried about you. Fritz and I left school right after homeroom and went looking for you. You should have come home."

I didn't say anything. I wished he hadn't taken Mr. Ohm. I hated to see my one good relationship with a teacher screwed up. But that didn't really matter now.

Dad went on, "Mr. Mattson came down to my homeroom and said he was suspending you for three days."

"It doesn't make any difference. I can't go back there now."

A long silence followed in the darkened room. I hunched deeper in the blanket.

"What are you going to do, then?"

"Just give me a little money and I'll go away and get a job."

"Where? What? You don't have any skills."

"I can do something with cars. Just so I'm out of here."

I waited for him to answer, listening to the clock drone its electric cycle.

Finally, he rose and walked heavily to the door. "Hungry?"

"No."

"Well, I'm going to make some soup and a sandwich. I'll bring you some. You don't have to eat it." Dad's silhouette looked stooped and old against the dim light from the living room.

I slept like I'd been drugged, the weight of my problems so overwhelming that sleep seemed the only refuge. In the morning I woke to find Dad standing by my bed in his school clothes. Fatigue was written in the dark rings under his eyes. He hasn't slept at all, I thought.

"Steven, I think you owe it to yourself to go back and get the credits you can. Things will be better next year."

I looked at him, trying to remember if I hated or loved him. "I can't, Dad."

"I think you can. You've got the whole week to think about it, anyway." For a long moment he hesitated. What did he want to say? Finally, he sighed. "Well, I've got to get to work. I'll see you tonight."

He left and I lay in bed trying not to think about yesterday. God, what an ass I'd made of myself. I tried every rationalization I could think of. They'd pushed me to it. Vanik and Cummings and Mattson and all the rest—especially Dad. But no matter how I blamed it on others, it always came back to me. I was the one who'd screwed up past imagining. Me! The Wart!

I shuffled around the apartment in my pajamas and bathrobe, trying to find something to take my mind off what had happened. It wasn't any good. My thoughts just wouldn't leave yesterday. Again and again I went over it, trying to find explanations, answers—hope.

Late in the morning I found myself standing by the corner table staring at the picture of Mom and Roxy. I'd tried to avoid thinking about them today more than ever, yet here I stood. I picked up the picture and gazed at it. What would that kind-eyed woman, that stranger from so long ago, have thought now? Would she have comforted me? Criticized me? Wept over me? How could I have faced her? I couldn't even look at her picture without wanting to cry. My world had disintegrated with the accident. Maybe it had never come back together, the pieces just flying farther away from that now-empty point in space where my world, our world, had once held together in orbit. If I'd only gone to Madison with them. . . .

I set down the picture so fast it tottered and fell on its back. What the hell had that meant! If I'd been along, there would now be three graves side by side on that hill in the cemetery. I stood looking at the toppled picture for a long moment. With shaking fingers, I set it upright, then turned and walked fast to the bathroom. I stood under a scalding shower for a long time, trying not to think of anything.

Dad called while I was getting dressed. He said he wanted to remind me there was chili in the refrigerator for lunch, but I knew his real reason was to make sure I was still there. I told him thanks and hung up. I was suddenly very hungry; I hadn't eaten since yesterday noon. I warmed up the chili and ate slowly. It was time to think clearly. What the hell was I going to do? I couldn't go back to school again. No way could I face that. Cripes, just imagine the crap Vanik, Cummings, and that bunch would give me now. My imagination was immediately off and running, and it took an almost physical effort to stop it. Steady, Wart. Stay calm.

I finished the chili, rinsed the bowl, and went out on our small balcony to smoke. Okay, I couldn't go back to school. Even if I could, without Capstone, it just wasn't worth it. But would Dad sign my withdrawal papers? It would be a great disgrace for him. Still, what else could he do? He couldn't actually make me go to school. I mean, they can't chain you to a desk, can they? It might be a long and nasty fight, but eventually he'd have to sign. Maybe I'd lie and tell him I'd go back next year. By then I'd have a job and enough money so no one could tell me what to do. Not Dad, not Mattson, not anyone.

But school was only part of it. Somehow, I had to get out of Brandt Mills. I wasn't going to stick around and run into kids from school all the time.

Maybe Keith and I could go away and find jobs in another town. Hell, they were about to kick him out of school anyway. Between us, we might have enough money to survive until we found work. I called his house, desperately hoping he'd returned. A surly voice answered on the fifth ring—Keith's dad. "Ya."

"Uh, hi. Is Keith home?"

"Who is this?"

"Steve Michaels. I'm a friend of Keith's."

"Well, Steve Michaels, friend of Keith's, my rotten son is not home. And he better not come home neither. You see him, you tell him his ass is grass if I ever see his face around here again." The line went dead.

I set the phone down slowly. So the Freakman was gone. Gone for good. Everything added up now: his quietness in the last few weeks, the "private things" he'd had to do on Friday, the way he'd said good-bye that afternoon. Well, good luck to him, I thought. I just wish he'd taken me with him.

I spent the rest of the afternoon trying to figure out how I was going to convince Dad. I rehearsed speech after speech. None of them sounded very convincing. Maybe in the end, I'd have to run away with the few lousy bucks I had saved.

He called again about four o'clock to tell me he'd forgotten that he had to give a report at a union meeting that night. Would I mind if he went? I told him no. I think we were both relieved at not having to spend the evening together.

About seven o'clock the phone rang again. I thought of ignoring it. I didn't want to talk to anyone. I didn't want anyone to know I was alive. But maybe it was Dad. After the fourth ring, I got up and walked slowly to the kitchen, hesitated, then picked up the receiver. "Hello."

74

"Hello, Steve? This is Trish. How are you?"

"Okay." Trish calling me? Why? What for?

"I just heard about it today. How are you feeling?"

"I said okay."

"I'm glad. I was worried. It's so unlike you to get so mad. I mean, you've always been so quiet. . . . Steve? Are you there?"

"Ya, I'm here."

Her words came in a rush. "Steve, what are you going to do?"

"I don't know. I'm suspended."

"But after that? I mean, we all know you're suspended."

"Why? Are all your friends eager to know?"

"Steve, that's not fair. I called because I care."

"I'm sorry. You caught me off guard. . . . I don't know. I guess I'm going to drop out."

"You can't do that, Steve."

"Why not? I'm going to fail half my courses anyway. Why should I stick around and take more crap?"

"Is it that bad?"

"Ya, it's that bad."

There was a pause. "Well, I don't think you should quit. If it makes any difference, I could help with algebra."

"Thanks, but it's a lot more than that. No way is Mattson going to pass me."

"But so what? You'll still have enough credits to be a junior."

"But I need a C average to get into Capstone, and if I can't get into Capstone, I don't want to go to school."

There was another pause, and when Trish spoke again, I thought I heard tears in her voice. "Well, I don't think you should drop out. I'm glad you're okay. 'Bye."

The line went dead and I stood there listening to the dial tone. I felt guilty for being grouchy. She hadn't had to call. I thought of calling her back to tell her thanks, but I didn't want to talk any more about school. Besides, what difference did it make? I'd never go back. Might as well forget the people too.

*   *   *

Dad got home late and I was afraid to leave my room to confront him with my decision. Even the best of my rehearsed speeches seemed puny now. I needed a few more hours to think—and to build my courage. I lay in bed with the lights off, listening to him moving around the apartment. On the way to his room, he hesitated at my door for a long minute, then walked slowly away. Good, no lecture tonight—but I felt myself wishing he'd just looked in to see if I was asleep.

Wednesday came. I saw Dad for only a few minutes in the morning and there was no time to talk about Monday or the future. Over breakfast I caught him watching me like I was some strange, incomprehensible specimen arrived in the mail, packed amid the usual frogs and worms, but somehow defying identification. When I met his eyes, he looked down quickly. In a minute, he excused himself, mumbling he was late for work.

He'd brought home my schoolbooks the night before and left them on the living-room table. But I didn't open them. I was done with school and schoolbooks. I needed to prepare for the big confrontation with Dad. And I was going to win this one.

I was still working on my speech when Dad called a little after three o'clock. "Steven, Mr. Mattson would like to talk to you at four-thirty. Just walk over; no one is going to see you. Everybody's long gone by four-thirty the night before convention."

"I can't, Dad."

There was a long pause. I heard him shift the phone to the other ear and sigh. "He's not really mad, Steven."

"I don't care about that."

There was another pause, then he said, "Steven, you've got to come. You can't have this hanging over your head forever. You've got to face him and square this. After that we'll talk about the future, but please do this."

I couldn't, I really couldn't, but he was right. "Will you

be there?" Was I asking my father for support? I couldn't believe it.

"Yes, I'll be there."

"Okay."

The sky was overcast and the smell from the mill hung in the air. I almost turned back a dozen times, but something stubborn inside me kept me walking. I was going to meet this head-on. Ya, I'd been wrong and I'd admit it. But I'd been pushed and it was time for everyone to see that. And I wasn't going back to school; that much I'd decided. If I could be calm and firm, then later Dad might sign my withdrawal papers. If he didn't, well, we'd have to get dirty.

But my courage washed away when I stepped into the square of light falling on the green carpet before the assistant principal's door. Mattson sat with his legs crossed on an open desk drawer, a half-smoked cigar in his stubby fingers. Dad sat with his chair close to the bookcases lining the opposite wall. A vacant, beige chair sat waiting midway between them.

"Sorry I'm late," I mumbled, slumping into the chair.

Neither one of them acknowledged my apology. Mattson straightened his chair, the springs making painful squeaking noises under his weight. He studied his cigar a moment before setting it carefully in an ashtray. "Your father tells me you want to quit school." I nodded; I couldn't trust myself to speak yet. "Well, I think your actions the other day were utterly reprehensible. Still, I don't want that incident to become an excuse for you to drop out."

"It's not just that. It's everything."

"What do you mean by 'everything'?"

I shrugged. "Just everything." My voice was hoarse. I wasn't doing very well on the dignified score. I knew his sharp blue eyes were probing me, but I didn't meet them.

"Mr. Lindon told me you were upset about something that happened in the cafeteria before class." I didn't answer. "Would you like to tell us about it?" I shook my head.

"Now and then some of the kids give Steven a hard time about being my son," Dad said.

"Was that it?" I nodded. "Who were the kids?"

"Some of the jocks."

Mattson snorted and I looked up in surprise to see him grind the cigar butt angrily into the ashtray. He shook his head, sighed, and got out a handkerchief to wipe the tobacco juice from his fingers. "I tell you, John," he said, looking over at Dad, "those kids are getting out of hand. Every year it seems to be worse—strutting around like they own the place. And half of them without the common sense of cabbages." He shook his head. "Sometimes I wonder if we don't do more damage than good with all the emphasis on sports."

"You won't get any argument from me on that one."

I was shocked. I'd always thought Mattson was a big fan. Hell, I'd seen him at every game I'd ever been to. Yet, here he was running down the jocks. I was suddenly off balance. Nothing was happening as I'd expected. Mattson waved a hand like he was brushing away a bothersome insect. "But that doesn't have much to do with what we were talking about. So, Steven, you had a run-in with some kids, got upset, and brought that to class with you."

"Sort of."

"Well, I don't think that excuses what you did, but I guess it makes it a little more understandable. I'm still going to fail you on the speech, but you can come back to school on Monday, and if you work hard, you can still pass my class."

That wasn't what I wanted! How could I ever face school again? I had come to apologize, then leave for good. I tried desperately to fill the silence that followed, but I could do nothing but stare wordlessly at him.

He went on. "I think you owe the class an apology. Nothing fancy, just stand up, say 'I'm sorry,' and sit down. In the future just try to keep calm."

Great words! Fine words! How the hell was I going to keep calm taking all the crap about being Wart, son of Toad? How was I going to keep calm when I was about to flunk half my courses? I looked from one to the other of them, but saw only satisfaction in their faces. This had all been planned in advance! Give the kid a mild reproof, follow it with a show of understanding, then offer forgiveness and another chance. And my real problems hadn't even been talked about! I was speechless. I'd been conned out of my socks.

Dad stood up and I numbly followed his example. At the door they shook hands. "Thanks, Dan. We appreciate it."

"No problem. We'll get things straightened out." Mattson turned to me, extending a hand. "And you have a good vacation, Steve. Don't worry about Monday; things happen sometimes. Try to get caught up in your studies."

I was trying with all my strength to get control of myself, to somehow tell them that this wasn't what I'd had in mind at all, but all I could do was mumble "I'm sorry."

He gave my hand a squeeze. "Of course you are. So am I. Let's just go on from here."

Dad was almost buoyant on the way home. He asked if I wanted to go out for dinner, but I said I had a headache. I spent the evening in my room trying to grasp how my life had suddenly turned about-face again.

8

The two days of teachers' convention had always been lazy for us. Even though teachers who didn't go to convention had to report to the school, no one, not even Dad, worried much about promptness. So, I figured that we'd sleep a little late Thursday morning. No such luck. It was still dark when a clatter of pots and pans woke me.

The clock on the kitchen wall read six-forty-five when I shuffled in and took my place at the table. Dad gave me a cheery good-morning and set waffles and bacon in front of me—my favorite breakfast. While I ate, he hovered around, asking if I had enough of this or that and making cheerful observations about the weather and spring coming soon.

His forced good humor drove me nuts and I hurried through breakfast. I had to get out of here and do some thinking. Long after he'd gone to bed I'd lain awake staring at the reflection of the streetlight on my ceiling. I'd finally made up my mind to tell him straight out that I wasn't going back to school. I'd explain my reasons carefully and maturely. If that didn't work, I was willing to fight.

But in the morning light my logic seemed much more fragile and my reasons far less convincing. And worse yet, there was a faint twitching of hope in the back of my mind. If I could just get into Capstone, I could make it through the last two years, graduate, and walk away, diploma in hand—it would prove they hadn't beaten me.

But they had beaten me. Why did I argue that? It was time to quit and get a job. But watching Dad cheerfully shoveling in waffles, I couldn't imagine how I was going to convince him. Hell, I'd never even had guts enough to tell him about my Capstone plans. I had to get away to think!

Yet, before I could push my chair back and ready an excuse, Dad started talking about his plan to bring up my grades. Between bites he outlined a schedule for the next four days that made a marine recruit's sound easy. I cringed. I was trapped. I'd either have to fight now or go along. My confusion boiled over. "I'm going for a walk first," I yelped, and jumped up from the table.

"Good idea. Good idea. Clear out the head a bit before work. I'll come with you. We don't have to go into school for a while yet."

"We?"

"Well, Steven, if I'm going to help you, you'll have to be nearby." And that way you'll also be able to check up on me, I thought bitterly. He finished a last bite of waffle, washed it down with coffee, and went to the closet for his coat.

What could I do now? I followed him listlessly down the stairs and out into the morning. For the first time in days hardly a breeze blew, but the sky still hung gray from horizon to horizon and I felt no trace of approaching spring.

Dad filled his lungs and let out a stream of frosty air. "Ah, spring is on the way. Can smell it already."

Horse crap, I thought.

After a few minutes of walking, he got back on the subject of school. "I went around and talked to your teachers yesterday. It seems to me that algebra is the big problem. You can understand what's going on in the other subjects, even if you've missed some work. You can catch up on them between now and finals and still pass, but you'll have to make up the algebra right away. Now, my algebra is a bit rusty, but I think I still remember most of it. I could tell from your test scores where you started to fall behind, so we'll start there and work through to the present. Four or five hours today, four or five tomorrow, and we'll get a long way." He tried to smile at me encouragingly. "Now, I picked up your other assignments too. When you get tired of math, you can work on them."

Tired of math! I'd been tired of math since fourth grade. But I didn't say anything. I was working up to the big speech. We'd followed a circular route around the quiet neighborhood and were only a block away from the apartment house. It was now or never.

"Dad, suppose I can't make it. Suppose it's too late." I took the plunge. "Maybe I should just quit now and save everybody the trouble. Let me have a couple hundred bucks and I'll go somewhere and get a job. I'll pay you back in a few months, I swear. . . . Maybe I'll go back to school next year," I finished lamely.

We were standing facing each other now. He was fighting hard for control. "Steven, you have *got* to try. All your teachers are willing to help. I'm willing to help. You have to be willing to help yourself. If you give it your best, you can make it. If you don't, you'll fail. But under no circumstances am I going to let you run away."

"Dad, it's not just the work, it's the whole school thing."

"Oh, you just let a little name-calling and ribbing get to you. That's silly. Just ignore them."

"You don't ignore them when they call you Toad. How am I supposed to ignore them when they call me Wart?"

His face got red. "That's an entirely different matter. When a student calls me . . . a name, he's striking at the very structure of the school. If I let him get away with it, pretty soon all the teachers will have nicknames. Then there will be no respect, no discipline, no education."

"So it's okay if Tom Vanik or one of the other jocks calls me Wart?"

"No, it's not okay, but you can afford to ignore them; I can't."

"I'd like to see you try to ignore Vanik if you were in my place. Hell, he'd kill me."

"Well, why do you make enemies of those boys? When you

hang around with a bunch of long-haired misfits, you just make yourself a target for abuse."

I fought to stay calm. "Dad, are you seriously telling me that Vanik and Cummings and their crowd are better than my friends? You're on the jocks all the time. I know. They make a point of telling me."

"Steven, don't deliberately misunderstand me. No, I don't like a lot about the jock crowd. I detest their arrogance. But at least they play by most of the rules. Your so-called dirts aren't good at anything and they ignore all the rules."

"Most of them don't call me Wart, Dad."

"And I'm telling you that neither would the jocks if you associated with a little better class of people."

"That's ridiculous, Dad." My voice was shaking now. "No one calls me Wart because I sit at the dirt table during study hall and lunch. It wasn't a jock who first called me Wart, it was a girl named Melissa. And it's not only the jocks who call me that now, it's almost everybody. Don't you know why, Dad? Do you really not know? It's because of you, Dad. It's because I'm your son. I'm the Wart, Dad. Wart, son of Toad!" I was yelling now.

He stood there, his face working. I didn't know what he was going to do—really start yelling or hit me or what. Finally he said with surprising calm, "Well, that doesn't justify dropping out of school or flunking algebra. You can't run away, Steven. You can't quit. You've got to go back to school and do your best no matter what anybody calls you . . . or me." We stared at each other. We'd gotten nowhere. It was impossible to communicate. I stood there with a thousand things in my head, but not one word on my lips.

Dad went on, his voice almost gentle. "Steven, remember your mother. She would have been very disappointed to see you quit school. She had great hopes for you, and I still do. Now, I know you've had a rough time, but it'll get better. I promise you it will. You've just got to have courage. Whenever you think of giving up, just think of her."

I turned away with tears burning in my eyes. I wanted to

scream, Why can't you just leave Mom out of it? My God, it's been three years! How long do we have to mourn? This is my life. Not hers. Not yours. Mine!

But I couldn't say anything. I started back for the apartment, my vision blurry as I fought back the tears.

I sat down at a lab table in Dad's classroom. He showed me where he thought I ought to start on the algebra, told me to call him when I got stuck, and went into his office. He was trying desperately to be calm and patient, and I knew my sullenness was stretching his resolve.

When he was safely out of sight, I put my head down on my arms and tried to think. I'd lost again. He'd thrown the one argument at me that I couldn't answer. How could I reply when he brought up Mom? Just the mention of her turned me to jelly. But I couldn't mourn forever. If he wanted to go on lighting his shrine to their memory every night for the rest of his life, let him, but I had to live my own life. Maybe I'd just run away. Better to starve in the street than face another Monday in school.

But there was still that tiny twitching of hope. Maybe I could still get into Capstone. After all, Mattson had said I could still pass his course. And history? I could make it there. Not easy, but I could. English? No big deal if I just made up my mind to do the reading. That left algebra. And there? Hell, it was impossible. There was just too much to do in too short a time. I was sunk. Quit now and spare myself the pain. I got up and trudged to the door to the hall. Where was I going? I didn't know. I returned to the table and wrote on a sheet of paper: "Dad, I've gone to the bathroom." I didn't say when I'd be back. Maybe I wouldn't be.

I walked slowly down the dim halls, the echo of my footsteps bouncing off the long rows of gray lockers. Eventually, my aimless route took me down into the vocational-arts wing. The light was on in the power shop and suddenly I wanted very much to talk to Mr. Ohm. I'd avoided even thinking about him since Monday when I'd heard him telling

Dad to take it easy on me. How embarrassing to know he'd been riding around with Dad looking for me. What had Dad told him in those three hours? Too much. More than I'd ever wanted Mr. Ohm to know about me. But now I wanted to talk to him. Perhaps he could help me convince Dad that I should drop out. Or maybe, just maybe, he'd agree to take me into Capstone even if I missed a C average. I knew the rules were very strict, but, my God, couldn't there be an occasional exception?

Mr. Ohm was sitting on a stool at one of the workbenches. "Hi, Mr. Ohm."

"Oh, hi, Steve. I didn't hear you come in. Be with you in a sec." He made a few more entries on a sheet in front of him. I took another stool and watched. "I've just been doing inventory, trying to figure out what tools we'll have to replace next year. I can never understand how so darn many tools get lost or broken. It's amazing." He finished and turned to me. "Well, how you doing?"

"Okay, I guess." Why did I always lie when somebody asked me that? I bent forward, looking at my hands.

"Good. . . . So, what brings you into school?"

"I'm doing some homework down in Dad's room."

"Getting caught up?"

I shrugged. I sure wasn't holding up my end of the conversation. I'd wanted to talk, so why didn't I talk? "I wanted to tell you thanks for helping Dad look for me on Monday."

"No problem. I found your dad and volunteered."

"How'd you hear about it so quick?"

"Skrypinski and another guy from your class told me."

"Ya. Probably laughing about it too."

"Not really. They were kind of concerned, I thought."

We sat for a minute in silence. "Mr. Ohm, suppose I don't quite get a C average, can I still get into Capstone on probation or something?"

He grimaced. "I wish I could tell you yes, Steve. If it was up to me, there'd be no problem, but the rules are set by the state. They're the same for all Capstone programs—secretarial, woodworking, whatever. We tried to get a waiver a couple of times for people in your situation, but"—he shrugged—"it was no soap. The Department of Public Instruction just wouldn't allow it."

I nodded, looking down at my hands again. Well, that question was answered; I was finished. I took a deep breath. "Well, there's no way I can get a C average, so I guess I'll quit."

"What does your dad say?"

I laughed and was surprised to hear how similar my laugh had become to Keith's bitter, humorless chuckle. "Oh, he thinks I should go on—become a doctor or a lawyer or something. I never even told him I wanted to sign up for Capstone—not that it makes any difference now."

"I think he already knows. He mentioned it while we were riding around Monday."

"He did?"

Mr. Ohm nodded. "He doesn't like it much, but he said if that's what it takes to keep you in school, he'd go along with it."

I was stunned. Dad knew? And he'd agree? "Why didn't he tell me?"

Mr. Ohm shrugged. "I don't know. You'll have to ask him."

I jumped up and started pacing. "That's just like Dad! Always fighting dirty. He's always pulling that kind of crap on me. He makes me beg and plead and even when he gives in, which isn't very damn often, it's only after he's got me crawling." I turned. "Do you know what he does when he can't find any other way to beat me?" I glared at Mr. Ohm, as if he was the one I was mad at. "He brings up Mom: be true to your mother's memory, remember your mother, your mother would be so disappointed, and on and on. Why can't he deal with me as I am? Why does he always . . ." I had both fists clenched trying to find the words. "Why does he always have to *dig her up?*"

Mr. Ohm sat motionless. At last he sighed and dug an old black pipe out of his overalls. He spent a long minute getting it filled and lighted, then he looked up at me. "I can't give you an answer to that, Steve. I'm sure he's unreasonable a lot of the time, but he's trying very hard—"

"To hound me to death."

Mr. Ohm smiled faintly. "It probably seems like that sometimes, but I wouldn't be quite so hard on him." He leaned forward, very serious. "Steve, I've known your dad for a lot of years. Maybe you've forgotten how different he used to be. Before the accident, I used to see a lot of him. We were on the same bowling team, and every couple of weeks five or six of us would play some cards." He paused. "But, after the accident, he changed. He quit bowling and playing cards. If he showed up for a faculty party, he'd only have a drink or two and leave. He always had the same excuse: he had to go home to be with you. Now, I hardly ever see him outside of school. I don't think anybody else does either."

"That's not my fault."

"Who said it was? I'm just telling you how it is." He paused again, studying the bowl of his pipe. "You say he fights dirty by bringing up your mother. Maybe so, but has it occurred to you that he lives his life trying to be true to her memory?" I sat back down and stared at the floor. "Has it?" Mr. Ohm asked gently.

"Ya, I guess."

"Steve, I can't tell you how to get along better with your dad. And I can't tell you what to do about school either. Personally, I think you ought to keep at it. In the long run, Capstone or no Capstone, I think it would be for the best. For you and for him. Now, that's my opinion and I'm not the smartest man in the world, but if you want it, there it is."

"Oh, here you are." Dad was at the door. He descended the four concrete steps to the floor of the shop.

Mr. Ohm turned. "Hi, John. Just been talking to your boy. Hope I didn't keep him too long."

"Not at all, Fritz, not at all." He was studying me, but he went on talking to Mr. Ohm. "Do you want to go out for some lunch in a couple of hours?"

"Sure. Why don't we try that new place south of town?"

I got up. "I'm going back to the room, Dad. Thanks, Mr. Ohm."

"Sure, anytime, Steve. Who else is around, John?"

I left them talking and went back to the biology lab. My books were lying where I'd left them, the English, the history, the damn algebra. I sat down and started the first problem on the open page of the algebra text. I couldn't make it, couldn't get the C average. But what else could I do right now but try to figure out the damn algebra? Later, when I could think straight, I'd make some decisions. Now I was just too damned confused.

Good humor doesn't come easy for Dad, but he made a valiant effort to keep it up all day. After lunch he spent over an hour demonstrating problem after problem from my algebra book as I watched dully. When I fumbled on the same or a similar problem, he'd take a deep breath and start again. About midafternoon he let me study some English instead, which was a bore, but better than algebra.

At home after supper, he gave me a ten-problem test he'd concocted and I failed miserably. Despite all the studying, my mind went blank the second I stared at the first problem. Hell, I'd done a dozen like it earlier in the day, but do you think I could remember how to now? No way.

Dad corrected my paper, his expression quickly becoming a scowl. Finally, he sighed. "Well, let's begin again." He put the paper in front of me. "Now watch, Steven." And his pen started moving, carefully and tightly, working out the answer to each problem in vivid red.

By ten-thirty Friday morning I was ready to scream, to beg for mercy. I went to the door to Dad's office. "Dad . . ."

He looked up from the stack of lab assignments he was correcting. "Stuck again?"

"No, it's going okay. I wondered if I could study at home the rest of the day."

"What's wrong with here?"

"I'm just sick of being in the school, Dad. I'll study at home, I really will." He sat tapping his infernal red pen and staring at me. "I promise, Dad."

He sighed. "All right. Show me your book." I got it and he flipped through the next twenty pages, then back a few. "Okay. I expect you to get to here by the time I get home. Is it a deal?" I nodded. "I won't be home for lunch. A few of us are going out. Do you want to meet us?"

"No, thanks, I'll warm up something at home."

Back at the apartment I plopped down in a chair and closed my eyes. A few hours of relief, thank God. I sat there maybe fifteen minutes letting my mind wander. I wanted to talk to someone, someone other than Dad, someone my own age. Keith was gone—gone for good. Who could I call? If there was just somebody who could help me with that damn algebra so I'd have it done when Dad came home . . . Trish? Ha! I had to be kidding. Trish come here? Fat chance! Still, why not ask? It would at least give me an excuse to talk to her. And maybe she would say yes. Crazier things had happened. After all, she'd called the other night and offered to help.

I almost hung up the phone when she answered. It was stupid to ask. I'd just be making a fool of myself again. "Hello, Trish, this is Steve."

"Hi, Steve."

"Uh, I wanted to thank you for calling the other night."

"That's okay. Are things better now?"

"A little, I guess. . . . Uh, you said you'd help me with the algebra. Does that still stand—"

"Sure. Do you want to see my assignment?"

"Well, I really need help with some of the earlier stuff."

"Oh, okay. When do you want to get together?"

"How about this afternoon?"

"Well, I'm not sure. Let me ask Mom." She was gone a couple of minutes. "She said it's okay. Do you still know how to find my place?"

"Well, you see, I'm still grounded, so you'd have to come over here."

"Oh . . . just a minute." She was gone two or three minutes. Why had I even asked? Dumb. "She said okay. I'll be over in half an hour or so."

I couldn't believe it. "Great! I really appreciate this, Trish."

I prowled around the apartment straightening up and then arranged my books and papers on the coffee table in front of the couch so it would look like I'd been working. Trish coming here! Algebra wouldn't be so bad with her sitting next to me. Nothing could be bad with her sitting next to me.

More like forty-five minutes passed before she got to the apartment. She apologized quickly and headed directly for the couch, the coffee table, and the algebra. Of course I was more interested in talking than math, but after bringing us each a Coke, I sat down and showed her my place in the book. She started explaining and demonstrating, but I was more aware of the sound of her voice and her body next to me than what she was saying. "Okay. You try one."

"What?"

"I said you try one. Come on, Steve, concentrate."

"Okay, okay. Let's see." I tried a problem and got part of it right. She went over the procedure again and I got it right the second time. But after that I let my mind wander again. I became aware of her perfume. Had she worn it for me? No, that was silly, but a nice fantasy anyway.

"Steve, you're not concentrating again."

"Sorry, I'll try harder." A few minutes later I let my arm drop from the back of the couch across her shoulders. She shrugged it away, but in a couple of minutes I put it back again and made a show of concentrating by saying, "Yes. . . . okay . . . ya, I got it."

She didn't shrug my arm away and I felt intoxicated, crazy thoughts reeling through my head. She talked steadily, carefully explaining each step of a long factoring problem. "There." She set down the pencil. "Now you try one." She turned to me, smiling.

I pulled her toward me. Both her hands shot up and pushed me away violently. "Steve!"

I sat looking at her in confusion. What had I been thinking? My God, I'd ruined everything! The look of surprise on her face changed to anger. She turned to the coffee table and snapped her book shut.

"I'm sorry," I said weakly.

"So am I, Steve. I thought you really wanted some help."

"I did. I do. I'm . . . I'm sorry."

She got up brusquely. "Well, good luck. I hope you make it."

"Trish, please don't go."

"I really have to, Steve. I was willing to help, but I don't have time to wrestle with you all afternoon."

My eyes were suddenly stinging with tears. God, not again! I turned away quickly.

"Steve?" Trish's voice had lost its anger.

I took a deep breath. Come on, Wart! Get control of yourself! No tears, damn it! I turned and tried to laugh. "I'm sorry. That was dumb." That was all I could say, and I had to look down.

She hesitated, then sat down on the edge of the couch. "Things are pretty awful, aren't they?"

I nodded. A minute passed before I could control my voice. "Ya, pretty awful." I took a deep breath and looked at her. "Hey, I'm really sorry. I don't know what I was thinking."

"It's okay. You just surprised me, that's all."

"Ya, I kind of surprised myself. I'm doing a lot of stupid things these days. I, ah, didn't plan this, you know. Don't tell anybody, okay?"

"No, of course not. Do you want to tell me what's going on?"

I looked down again. "You don't want to hear about it."

"Yes, I do. Go ahead. Tell me."

And I did, dragging up all my hurts, fears, and my last few fragile dreams about Capstone, graduation, and escape. She listened, asking a question now and then, but mostly just listening and nodding her head. I talked almost nonstop for an hour and a half. Finally I stopped and we sat looking at each other. She leaned over and hugged me quick. "I've got to go."

She got up and went for her coat. At the door I handed her books to her awkwardly. "I'm sorry about everything."

"It's okay. Don't worry about it. I feel complimented you could talk to me. And I know you can work it out, Steve. I know you can make it."

"Well, thanks for coming. I really didn't ask you to come over so I could, uh, you know . . ."

"So you could seduce me?" She giggled and I blushed. "That was kind of a compliment too." She was serious. "And maybe I would have felt differently about it, but you see, I met a boy last summer when I was working at the camp and, well, we're writing and I'm pretty serious about him. You can understand that, can't you?" I nodded. "Good. I'll see you in school." She stood on tiptoes and gave me a hug. The door swung in.

"What the hell is going on here?"

"Dad! You're early."

"Good of you to notice. And this is what you wanted to come home for? This is how you study algebra?"

"Dad, she was helping me."

"So I see." He bowed with mock courtesy, sweeping his arm toward the door. "Young lady, if you don't mind. I'm sure my son found your instruction most interesting. If you make a practice of being alone in apartments with boys, I'm sure you must have many requests for tutoring."

"Now hold on, Dad." He turned to me, eyes blazing, but I met them. "You can't talk to her that way. Whether you believe it or not, nothing happened."

"Steven, if your mother—"

"Oh, don't give me that crap." His fists doubled up and he took a step my way. "Go ahead, Dad, hit me. That'll solve a lot."

"Steve, Mr. Michaels, please!" Trish's voice was almost a scream. We turned to her, surprised. For a few seconds we'd both forgotten she was there. She looked from one to the other of us, then started crying and ran from the apartment.

For a few more seconds we stood silent, then I exploded. "Real good, Dad. That was about the most decent person I know, about the best friend I've got. Do you want to call her a whore again?" I stood with my fists clenched. He looked at me in confusion. "Anytime, Dad. You just call me and we'll discuss it in detail." I raised my fists. "Anytime, Toad."

We stared at each other for a long moment, then I spun and stalked to my room, slamming the door behind me.

9

I was lying on my bed, my rage still simmering, when Dad knocked on my door an hour later. "Go away."

"Steven, I want to talk."

"I don't. We have nothing to say to each other, Dad."

There was a pause. "I want to apologize to that girl, Steven, but I don't know her name."

Well, Trish deserved that anyway. "Her name is Trish McIntyre. Her father's name is Patrick. He's in the phone book."

"Can we talk for a minute first?"

"Oh, all right. Come in." I sat up and leaned back against the headboard, folding my arms.

Dad sat down on my chair. "I shouldn't have said some of those things to her."

"That's right, Dad, you shouldn't have."

"But what was I supposed to think when I came home and found my son in the arms of a girl?"

"You might have interpreted it as a friendly gesture, which was all it was. You might have listened to me."

"Now just a minute, Steven! I'm not going to take all the blame for this. I'm still very upset about you lying to me this morning."

"Lying about what?"

"About coming home to study."

"That wasn't a lie. Do you think I had this planned in advance?"

"Didn't you?"

"No, Dad, I didn't. I didn't even think of calling her until after I got home. And she was nice enough to come over to work on algebra with me. And that's what we did, Dad, we worked." Dad opened his mouth. "Let me finish. Now, I'll admit we didn't work very long, because I needed to talk about things important to me. And she listened, Dad, which is more than you ever do."

He was getting angry again. "That's not true, Steven. You've always had an opportunity to talk in this house. Ever since your mother was—"

"There you go bringing her up again."

There was a long pause, then Dad said very quietly, "And what's wrong with that?"

For a moment I was afraid of him. There was something dangerous in his tone, a knife edge behind the quiet words. When I spoke again, I tried to take the anger out of my voice without letting the fear creep in. "I loved Mom and Roxy too, Dad. I just don't need to be reminded of them every time we disagree."

There was another pause before he spoke again. "I see." His voice was still soft, but the tone was different. We sat for a couple of minutes in silence, then he got up. "I'm going to call your friend." At the door he turned. "I still don't think you should have invited her over. I may have overreacted, but it didn't look very innocent when I came in. And I doubt if her parents would have approved of her being alone in an apartment with a boy."

"I was alone with her on a date once, Dad. How was that different?"

He shook his head. "Well, we'll talk more later. I see a considerable difference, even if you don't. What kind of people are her parents?"

"Why," I said sarcastically, "are you afraid they've called

the principal or the superintendent of schools?" That was a low blow and I could see it hit home. I relented. "I doubt if she told them, Dad. She wouldn't want to make trouble for you or me."

He nodded and left the room. I got up and went to the door so I could listen. I heard him turn the pages of the phone book, then dial. "Hello, is this Trish McIntyre? . . . This is Mr. Michaels. I want to apologize for what I said this afternoon. . . . Yes, I know you were just trying to help Steven. I just misread the entire situation and I do apologize. . . . Thank you. . . . Yes I know he's having a difficult time. I also know that sometimes I make it harder for him. I appreciate your willingness to help. . . . No, he's not too upset now. We just had a talk and I think things are a little better. . . . Yes, I hope so too. . . . Good. I appreciate that. . . . Thank you again, Trish. I really am sorry about this afternoon. Good-bye."

I went back and sat on my bed again. It had been good of Dad to apologize. In a lot of ways he hadn't had to. After all, things probably had looked damn strange when he walked in. And, I reminded myself guiltily, his suspicions hadn't been exactly unfounded. If I'd had my way, the afternoon would have been considerably less innocent. I felt a surge of jealousy: I wanted to be the guy she'd met last summer.

Dad knocked on the doorjamb. He had his overcoat on. "I picked up a present for you at noon." He handed me a square package about the size of a book, wrapped in white tissue paper. "I hope you'll still want it."

I held it awkwardly. "Thanks."

"I'm going to get a bucket of chicken. I don't feel much like cooking tonight." He left quickly.

I slowly unwrapped the package. It was a framed picture of Mom and Roxy identical to the one on the corner table in the living room. The two smiling faces stared up at me and I felt like crying all over again. I'd tried to tell myself a million times that I was over it, that I was done mourning, that my mother and sister were now just fading images in a picture. But they weren't, damn them! They were more, much more. And I couldn't escape them, no matter how hard I tried.

When Dad got back with the chicken, I was working on the algebra. I'm not sure how or why I'd made the decision to stay in school. The picture hadn't convinced me. No one's arguments had convinced me. Getting into Capstone was almost out of the question and even the thought of next Monday filled me with terror. Still, I was going to give it one final shot.

We ate dinner without talking, both of us making a show of concentrating on the TV news. After dishes I went back to my room and the algebra. With the help of the examples Trish and Dad had given me, I finally started getting the hang of the factoring. About nine o'clock I went out to the kitchen for a Coke. Dad had some work spread out on the table.

"Anything I can do to help, Steven?"

"No, thanks, Dad. I'm doing okay." I paused on my way out. "Thanks for the picture, Dad. That was nice of you."

"You're welcome. Let me know if I can help."

I had to ask. It had been bothering me since I'd talked to Mr. Ohm on Thursday. "Dad, why didn't you tell me you knew I wanted to sign up for Capstone and were even willing to go along with it?"

"Did Fritz tell you that?" I nodded. Dad took off his glasses, polished them, and put them back on. "I guess because I disapproved and still hoped to talk you out of it."

"Well, you don't have to worry about it anymore. I need a C average to get in and I won't have one. But you would have signed?" He nodded. "And if by some unbelievable luck I do get a C average, you'll still sign?"

"Yes."

"Why, Dad? That goes against everything you've ever said about school."

"Well, I guess I'd sign hoping you'd reconsider in a year or so."

"I wouldn't, Dad. I'm not going to college. I'm not like you. I'm going to be a mechanic."

We looked at each other. He compressed his lips, then shrugged. "Well, better that than a dropout, I guess."

"Auto mechanics is what I like, Dad. It's what I'm good at. . . . I've got to get back to the algebra."

At my desk, I turned to the next chapter. Damn it! If I'd just known a few weeks earlier, maybe I could have made it. Why the hell hadn't he told me? It was just as bad as lying. It was lying. He'd known and hadn't told me he'd sign! The point of my pencil snapped under the pressure of my hand and I slapped the pencil down and sat fuming. And why hadn't I brought it up when there was still time? He couldn't be honest with me and I couldn't be honest with him. We were the same: the Wart and the Toad. Damn.

All weekend I worked, my energy born of anger and desperation, no real hope. By Sunday night I had a brutal headache, but perhaps the faintest gleam of hope had begun to penetrate my gloom. If I could just get D's, then at least I wouldn't have to take the courses over.

Although I was still mad at Dad, I'd asked his help several times on Saturday and Sunday. His patience had stretched pretty thin a couple of times when I'd screwed up on simple problems, but we'd made it through without any more yelling.

I was surprised how little notice everyone took of me Monday morning. A couple of kids from speech class looked at me funny and there were the usual "Hi ya, Wart" calls in the hall, but nothing major. My teachers, if they knew the reason for my suspension (and I was sure they all did), acted as if nothing had happened. At noon I stayed in the library rather than chance a confrontation with any jocks in the cafeteria.

This was my day for auto mechanics and I felt a great relief when I came into the shop. The starter I'd been working on still lay where I'd left it, and I got so involved fixing it that all my troubles drained away.

Tuesday was going to be a bummer. I studied my butt off Monday night, trying to forget that I'd have to apologize to the speech class on Tuesday afternoon. Even doing algebra was better than thinking about that.

Although Mattson had said it didn't have to be anything fancy, I was already mentally rehearsing my lines when I got to gym late Tuesday morning. We played water polo, a tough, violent game with over forty kids in the pool. I stayed down in the deep end with the better swimmers where I could handle myself and not get my head kicked in. Jeff was treading water near me, but Perry was down in the shallow end where the action was much heavier—lots of flailing elbows, bumped heads, and bruised lips.

Jeff said, "I hope Perry stays cool. He takes this damned stuff too serious."

"Ya," I said, "all I want to do is stay alive."

"Me, too. This is nuts. Just too many guys."

We watched Perry fight his way into a knot of kids and come out with the ball. "Damn, he really is into this," I said.

"Ya, and he's speeding too. Here we go." The ball came our way. Jeff had it in three strokes and flipped it back to me. I hurled it in the general direction of our goal at the head of the deep end. No fancy teamwork for this boy. I wasn't holding on to the ball any longer than I had to.

My shot was about eight feet wide and a guy from the other team intercepted it and passed it back into the shallow end. Most of the jocks in the class had gotten on the other team and were trying to organize a coordinated push on our goal. Our defense was chaotic but determined, and three more times got the ball back into deep water. Neither Jeff nor I handled the ball those times, but I saw Perry working hard on the perimeter of our defense around the goal.

The fourth or fifth time the jocks mounted an attack, Fred carried the ball. He came in behind four other big guys, stiff-arming Perry out of the way. Perry stumbled back, then surface-dived against the back of Fred's knees. Fred staggered, passed the ball off, then fell backward on top of Perry. He lumbered up, holding Perry under with a big right hand, slipped, and fell on him again. By the time Fred finally got to his feet, Perry had been under a very long time. He burst to the surface, choking and gagging. His forehead had been scraped raw where Fred's weight had twice slammed him against the bottom. Half-drowned, he lurched to the side of the pool just as one of the jocks finally scored.

Jeff and I didn't have any time to worry about Perry for the next few minutes, because the goals switched with the score and things got a lot hotter for us real quick. Still, we managed to keep from getting killed, handling the ball a couple of times, but passing it off before too many big bodies plunged our way.

Perry already had his clothes on and a Band-Aid on his forehead when the rest of the class got into the locker room. Fred saw him and yelled, "Hey, dirt, you got an owwie? Gonna take it home to Mommie and have her kiss it?" Several of the jocks laughed. Perry didn't say anything, just glared at them and slammed out the door.

Jeff was dressing next to me. "Perry sure got his this time," he said.

"Ya. Too bad, but he ought to know better. Fred is only twice his size and three times as strong."

Jeff nodded. "Ya, but that's Perry. Just a hotheaded little shit. This ain't the first time or the last." He sighed. "Well, I'm gonna go find him before he hypes out."

"Good luck." Maybe I should have gone with him, but I figured there might be more trouble and I wanted no part of it. I had enough trouble with the jocks already.

I had to go to the can, so the lunch lines were already pretty long by the time I got to the cafeteria. Perry and Jeff came in from the smoking lounge and headed for the shorter line forming at the other end of the cafeteria. Perry looked grim, but okay.

My mind was back on speech and I was again rehearsing my apology as I got close to the head of the line. Jeff had just turned from his line and was looking for a place to sit. Perry was picking up his last dish when Fred walked past, following

Vanik and Cummings. They were laughing, acting the big shots, as always.

I don't know what Fred said, even Jeff never knew. Maybe Fred didn't say anything, but suddenly Perry whirled and smashed tray, plate, bowls, and food against the back of Fred's head. Fred went down hard and Perry was at him, kicking at his head. One of the cooks started screaming and there was lots of yelling, then Perry was running down the center aisle, heading for the doors to the parking lot. He dodged one of the supervisors by jumping on top of a table and leaping to the next, kicking dishes and trays out of his way. His eyes were crazy and his mouth was open in a kind of soundless scream. He hit the doors and was through. Jeff came running after him, skidded on some spilled food, and fell. A couple of the supervisors dashed out the doors, but Perry was long gone.

Maybe it was the speed he'd done that morning, or maybe the whole damn jock/dirt thing just finally got to him. Nobody ever really figured it out.

Perry jumped in his car, roared out onto Piersal Street, and three blocks away ran a stoplight right in front of a pulp truck headed for the mill. The newspaper said he was killed instantly.

10

The flag outside the administration wing flew at half-mast for the rest of the week. Trish caught me in the hall Friday morning and asked if she and a couple of her friends could get a ride with us to the funeral that afternoon. I said sure, and the girls met us in the parking lot a little before two o'clock. Dad and Trish were polite, almost friendly.

Quite a few people from the school were at the funeral—not a majority or even a quarter, but more people than had ever paid much attention to Perry when he was alive. Mattson and the Phantom were there near the front, looking pious and dignified. It irked me that they had found places so close to Perry's family. Hell, probably neither one of them had even known Perry's name.

The five of us took a pew near the back. This was the first funeral I'd been to since Grandma's a few months after Mom and Roxy's. Bad memories, times I tried not to think about. I looked around for Jeff. I didn't see him anywhere in the crowded church. Maybe he was one of the pallbearers. That would only be right, although I wasn't sure how he'd bear up. He hadn't been in school since Tuesday.

I didn't see Jeff until the service was about to begin. He stood in a corner of the vestibule at the rear of the church, dressed in jeans and a wool shirt. The light from the small stained-glass window near him lit his anguished face with shades of red and gold. I got by the three girls to the aisle as quietly as I could and slipped into the vestibule. "Jeff, come sit with us." He shook his head. "Come on, Jeff. We're all friends of yours."

"I'm not dressed for it."

"No one will care. . . . Jeff, I know it's tough. I had to go to my own mother and sister's funeral. But it's something you have to do."

"I can't."

"Jeff, you've got to say good-bye. He was your best friend."

He turned tormented eyes on me. "I just can't do that." He spun and plunged out the door, down the steps, and past the hearse where they were lifting out Perry's casket. The minister, the funeral director, and the pallbearers turned in surprise to look after the boy who ran very fast down the sunlit April street.

The girls all cried during the service, but I tried to submerge my emotions. How senseless and cruel Perry's death had been. Yet even more powerful than my outrage was the memory of that other funeral where I'd stood next to Dad, staring at the two closed caskets hiding all that remained of my mother and my sister. But I couldn't let myself think of that now. In another few weeks Dad and I would go through the annual ritual of remembering their deaths. I wasn't strong enough to do it here among all these people.

Once or twice I glanced at Dad. His face was expressionless, but what were his thoughts?

The interment service was for the family only, so a lot of people stood around outside the church after the funeral watching the tail end of the small procession slowly pull out and head down through town. I wondered where Jeff had gone. If I'd known, maybe I would have gone to comfort him, taken some responsibility, as I should have when he'd gone to talk to Perry outside the locker room.

Dad said, "I'm going to walk back to the school. I don't mean to be disrespectful to your friend, kids, but I've got some work I have to do. Can you drive the girls home, Steven?"

"Sure. Are you going to walk home or should I come by the school?"

"It's supposed to cloud up and rain. You'd better pick me up around five." He set off, but his pace was slow and I knew he was thinking—remembering—not hurrying off to get his work done.

I dropped off Beth and Carol, then asked Trish if she'd like to go for a ride in the country. She said that would be okay and I drove out of town along the river. The snow still lay in the woods and shady places, but the fields were almost bare. The ice on the river was breaking up, a deep black channel slowly widening as the ice along the shores slipped away in big chunks.

The land seemed to reflect our mood. There was no hint of green on the hills and fields, just browns, blacks, and dirty whites. The sky was clouding over fast, the blue turning to ash. Where the narrow county road swings down near the river about five miles from town, I pulled in at a wayside and turned the car around.

"Let's get out for a minute," Trish said.

We sat on a rickety picnic table beside the river. The breeze was chilly and we pulled our coats tighter about us and sat close, not girlfriend and boyfriend, just friends.

"Why didn't Jeff come in?" she asked.

"He just couldn't take it, I guess."

"Why did Perry do it? I heard about the water-polo game, but why did he, you know, hype out?"

"I don't know. I guess he just got pushed too hard."

"I was in health with him last year. He didn't like Mr. Peterson much. They used to fight."

"Ya, Jeff called Perry a 'hotheaded little shit.' He always kind of had a chip on his shoulder."

"Why was he like that?"

"Hell, I don't know. I'm no shrink." I thought for a minute. "I just wish . . ."

"What?"

104

"I just wish I'd talked to him after gym. Jeff went to tell him to cool off, but I didn't want to get involved."

"Well, Jeff was closer to him than you were."

"I know, but maybe if I'd gone with Jeff to talk to him, it wouldn't have happened."

"I don't think you should blame yourself. It wasn't anyone's fault."

"Well, Fred sure as hell had something to do with it."

"I suppose so, but I don't think he wanted something like that to happen. He's looked pretty unhappy the last couple of days."

"Ya, but you didn't see him at the funeral, did you? Or Vanik or Cummings or any of the other jocks? They probably played basketball after school."

"You really hate those guys, don't you?"

"Why shouldn't I, the way they're always laying crap on me and the other dirts?"

"You're not a dirt. You don't walk around with your jacket on all the time and your shirt half-unbuttoned. Your hair isn't even very long."

"Well, I'd have a lot more hair if Dad would let me."

"Maybe, but I bet you'd never really join that group. You're too much of an individualist for that."

I looked at her in surprise. Was that what she thought? I wasn't any big individualist by choice. I was a loner because I'd never felt particularly welcome in any group—even the dirts.

I shrugged. "Well, I'm more a part of that group than any other. I'll side with them any day against the jocks or the administration." I paused, my anger rising. "And I blame the administration a lot for what happened to Perry. I mean, everyone knew about the jock/dirt thing, but do you suppose anyone bothered to do anything about it? Hell, if the jocks had been laying crap on the kids in National Honor Society or the kids in band or drama, the administration would damn well have done something. But for dirts?" She tried to interrupt, but I was good and steamed up now. "I mean, did you see Mattson and the Phantom standing there this afternoon, looking oh so pious and sorrowful? Lot of damn good that does now. And just wait and see. Everything will be back to normal next week. Everybody will just go on playing games and the administration will look the other way until it happens again."

I paused, fuming.

Trish said quietly, "I think you're too hard on people. I think things will settle down. I don't think anybody is going to forget Perry that fast."

I sat for a long minute with my eyes closed. Why was I yelling at her? Finally, I said, "I hope you're right."

She took my hand. "Come on. Let's walk a little bit. I'm cold." We walked in silence along the riverbank. Nearly submerged chunks of ice floated downstream in the cold, dark channel, gouging and grinding against the weakening shore ice. In another few days the whole river would flow free of ice—spring, a time for new beginnings, but I felt no elation, no promise of better times ahead.

Trish started talking about other things, asking me the same questions everyone else seemed to ask. I really didn't feel like talking about school or Dad this afternoon. Still, I appreciated her concern and tried to sound more cheerful. After a few minutes we returned to the car and drove back into town through the early dusk, the brown hills and fields on one side, the dark, cold river on the other.

Dad and I passed the weekend quietly. In the aftermath of Perry's tragedy, I found having homework almost a relief.

In Mattson's class on Monday, we began impromptu speeches, a unit everybody looked forward to about as much as having wisdom teeth pulled. For me it was going to be doubly bad. In the previous week's commotion, Mattson had forgotten to give me a chance to apologize to the class for throwing the brick. Now I might have to apologize and give a speech on the same day.

Mattson came in as the bell rang, and took attendance. Jeff's chair was vacant. I'd seen him in the hall earlier in the day, but I couldn't blame him for skipping class. The speaking order and the topics for the impromptus would be picked by chance. What incredible pressure a little bad luck might put on Jeff.

My own luck ran true to form. We chose numbers from a jar to determine the speaking order and when I unfolded my slip, I found a big red 1. The luck of the Wart.

"Who has number one?" Mattson asked. I raised my hand. "Very well, Steve, choose a picture. The rest of you read your assignments and give Steve a chance to think."

I got up and went to select one of the 8 × 10 pictures lying facedown on the table at the front of the class. I wonder if he remembers about the apology, I thought. Maybe I can just skip it. No, better not. I turned over the picture. An Italian guy in a red striped shirt and a chef's hat was throwing a pizza crust as a half-dozen little kids watched in wonder. The pizza man was grinning beneath a huge curled mustache.

I got back to my seat. Mattson pushed the button on his stopwatch. I now had a single short minute to make up a two-minute story about the picture. What the hell was I going to say? My mind bounced from one thing to another, but nothing sounded good. A pizza chef was throwing a crust while some kids watched. What more could one say? Kids, pizza, Italian, mustache, apology. . . .

"Time. Steve, the floor is yours."

I got up numbly and went to the podium. All the kids were watching me with extra attention. How was the Wart going to screw up this time? It was sure to be interesting.

"A person . . ." My voice sounded like I'd swallowed a dishcloth, and I cleared my throat. "A person can throw many things." There were a couple of giggles immediately and I felt a big drop of sweat roll down my side. Oh, hell, great choice of words, Wart! "Baseball pitchers throw baseballs, quarterbacks throw footballs, and basketball players throw basketballs. When you make a pot, that is called throwing a pot." I hesitated, then stumbled on. "We all enjoy people who throw parties. These things are all good things to throw. But people shouldn't throw food, like sometimes happens in the cafeteria." There were a couple of laughs. God, this was awful. "Yes, food fights get lots of people upset, like the cooks, the janitors, and the administrators, especially if one of them happens to get hit with a meatball or something." More laughs. Where the hell was this supposed to lead? "Anyway, I think we'll all agree that throwing food isn't a good idea unless"—I held up the picture so the class could see—"you happen to be a pizza cook. That's what this man is, and it's okay to throw food if you're making a pizza crust, although you've got to have lots of practice to do it right, just like throwing a football or something. And, well"—my face was burning and the picture trembled in my hands—"there are some other things you can throw, but shouldn't—like bricks and tantrums. And I'm sorry I did that and I apologize."

I hurried back to my seat, not looking at anybody. It had been much too short. To my surprise there was a brief flutter of applause.

"Thank you, Steve," Mattson said. "Fill out your critique sheets, class. We won't take time for oral critiques today. Who has number two?"

Hal raised his hand, got up, and went to choose his picture. While he thought and the other kids filled out their critiques, I sat staring at my desktop. I'd screwed up again! How stupid it had all sounded. God, had Mattson thought I was making fun of the administrators with that line about getting hit with a meatball? Damn. He was going to flunk me surer than hell.

"Time. You have the floor, Hal."

Hal spoke, smooth and confident. Other kids followed. I filled out my critique sheets listlessly. Ten minutes from the end of the class, Mattson collected them and told us to read our textbook assignment. I tried, but couldn't concentrate. Maybe he'd give me a D. I mean, I'd made it through, hadn't I? That was at least something.

The bell rang. "Steve, wait a minute, please." The rest of

the class left, a couple of the kids glancing behind. Mattson handed me my grade report. "I thought you'd like this now." He left the room, heading for his office and his disciplinary chores.

I unfolded the sheet. "The assignment stipulated a story, and stories require plots. Your speech was only a list of examples of what can be thrown actually and figuratively. However, your example of throwing a pot was good. Also, you rather ingeniously (and courageously) incorporated your apology into your speech. Your nervousness was quite apparent, but understandable under the circumstances. Generally a good job. C+."

I almost whooped. Hell, I would have settled for a D!

On the walk home from school I was still elated. I knew it was no big deal; a C+ on a small speech wouldn't raise my grade even close to passing. Still, it was a start, and I'd finally made my apology. I'd gotten a C and a C+ on tests in history and English in the last few days. Hell, I'd even passed an algebra quiz with four out of five points. Taken altogether, the grades probably didn't improve matters very much. Yet, not all was darkness.

I remembered a little guiltily that Perry hadn't been buried three days and here I was strolling along feeling pretty damned good. Still, it was a beautiful spring day and I did feel good. I even allowed myself a faint optimism about Capstone. Maybe it was still possible to get a C average. The chances were damned remote, but maybe, just maybe . . . I quickened my step. I had a lot of work to do.

For the next three weeks I busted my ass studying. Not that I'd turned into a model student or anything. I still hated the work, but I'd gotten stubborn and kept pushing. In school I stayed as much to myself as possible, studying in the library or a vacant classroom and walking home right after dismissal. The weather continued beautiful as we got well into April and I enjoyed the exercise and fresh air before the long evenings of homework.

Now and then I'd ask Dad for help on the algebra, but mostly I worked by myself, ignoring him when he checked up on me with this or that flimsy excuse. It was almost funny; my new-found studiousness left him confused. Still, as long as I plugged away at the books, he bent over backward to be agreeable. At school he was still the same old Toad and twice more notes appeared on the windshield of the Buick, but by now they seemed empty threats and Dad contemptuously ignored them.

Trish had been right about things cooling down. The Phantom had made a bland statement during morning announcements on the Monday following Perry's funeral. He said the school had "lost one of its own" and we should all "mourn and work together." I don't think anyone paid any attention to him. Since when had the Phantom known anything? Still, by what seemed mutual consent, jocks and dirts ignored one another. I distanced myself from the whole thing. With Keith gone, Perry dead, and Jeff avoiding everyone, I didn't feel much like associating with anybody. I had my own problems.

A lull came in the Wart crap. I still heard it in the halls, but it was usually more of a greeting than anything else. That way I could take it. Only when I was unfortunate enough to run into Vanik or Cummings or one of their crowd was I likely to hear the word with a different edge. And even they didn't seem very interested in abusing me at the moment.

By mid-April things were going about as well as I could remember. Dad and I weren't fighting. My grades were coming up a little. I talked to Trish on the phone every couple of nights, and even if she was never going to be my girlfriend, at least she was my friend and enjoyed talking to me too.

And the end was in sight. No matter if I passed all my courses or not, summer vacation was only six weeks away. I counted the days, even the hours.

Everything started to go to hell again in the third week in April. Rounding a corner on a Tuesday morning, I found Dad pushing a kid against a locker. "What did you call me, young man?" His voice was brittle.

"Nothin'. I didn't call you nothin'."

"Oh, you didn't, huh? Then who was it who shouted 'Hey, Toad'?"

"Not me. It was one of them." He gestured at three kids slowly retreating down the hall.

"You're lying! I was looking right at you."

"The hell . . ." The kid tried to pull away, but Dad slammed him back against the locker. "You son of a bitch, get your hands off me." He started to swing at Dad, but Dad is a lot quicker than he looks and, hooking the kid's leg, sent him sprawling to the floor.

"Do you want to try that again?" He stood threateningly over the kid. The kid didn't reply, just glared up at Dad, then past him at me. "Come on, youngster, let's go to the office. I don't think you want another round."

The kid got up and Dad grabbed his arm, but he pulled away and Dad let him follow sullenly behind. At the next corner the kid turned for a second and gave me the finger. Hell, I didn't even know him. But I guess that didn't make any difference. He knew Dad. And he knew me.

That night Dad replayed the scene over dinner, but I didn't acknowledge that I'd seen it all. Somehow Dad hadn't noticed me, so wrapped up in his anger that he hadn't even looked around. Mattson had suspended the kid for three days and Dad took satisfaction in that. Since the conference ending my suspension, he'd reversed his opinion of Mattson and now praised him at every opportunity. After dinner I retreated to my room, glad to have homework to do.

The week ran on without further incident and I almost forgot about the whole thing. The kid's suspension was up on Friday. Thursday after school Dad, Mattson, the kid, whose name I'd found out was Greg Demer, and his parents met for a conference. Apparently no fireworks exploded and Dad was in a good mood on the ride home.

The teachers' union was having a supper that night, so I ate alone, did the dishes, and then got at the books for a couple of hours before turning on the TV for a movie. Three weeks of hard studying had put me in pretty good shape in nearly everything. Algebra was still shaky and I had makeup work to do in the other classes to be ready for finals, but for once I thought I could afford a break.

The movie was okay, nothing special really, but I enjoyed putting my feet up and forgetting about school for a while. The thought of meeting Greg in the halls bothered me a little, but not too much. His parents had sided with Dad, so he'd probably just be sulking.

About nine-thirty I was thinking about making some popcorn for the last half-hour of the movie. I'd just about pried myself out of the easy chair when I heard Dad's key in the front door. Maybe he'd like some too. I was feeling downright sociable and turned to ask him when he came in from the kitchen. The look on his face stopped me.

"What is that TV doing on?"

I stumbled. I couldn't think how to reply. "Well, I don't know, there was a good movie on—"

"I don't care what was on. I made a rule about TV and I don't expect you to forget it." He marched over to the TV and shut it off with a vicious slap of his hand.

The rule! Hell, I'd forgotten completely about the rules Dad had laid down when he'd grounded me. So much had happened since then. He turned and stood, hands on hips, glaring at me.

"Dad, I forgot all about it. I studied for a while and then sat down to take a break. It was no big deal."

He was steaming. "Ya, ya, I know. Just sat down for a break. And I thought you'd learned enough responsibility in the last few weeks so I could go out for three or four hours. But I guess I was wrong. I'll just have to sit here every evening and baby-sit you for the rest of the year." He stomped into the kitchen.

I sat stunned. So he really thought all my progress had been due to his silly rules. He'd given me no credit at all. Almost choking on my anger, I stalked to my bedroom. Nothing would have given me greater pleasure than to follow him to the kitchen and have a scene then and there, even if it came to blows, but I wasn't going to do it. No, I'd broken free of him, of Mattson, of all of them. I'd counted up the score, figured my goal, calculated the odds, and discarded everything that was needless. I was going to make it, not for them, but for myself. And everything and everybody else could go to hell.

I grabbed the top book on my pile and slapped it open to the last page I'd read. Screw 'em, I thought, just screw 'em all. I read savagely, slashing down the paragraphs, snapping back one page after another, grabbing every fact and swallowing it. I needed to remember this crap just long enough to pass finals. In the summer I was getting the hell out of this place—maybe forever.

All Friday Dad's words stuck in my mind. How on earth could he interpret the last weeks that way? Damn it, I was going to show him! I was going to show everybody that I could make it on my own. I didn't need anybody's stinking rules.

At lunch I saw Greg and a couple of his friends hanging around the jock table. That placed him for me. I'd seen him sucking up to Cummings, Vanik, and their crowd before. Quite a few kids liked to stick close to the jocks. I guess you could call them groupies. They were too small or didn't have the talent to be jocks themselves, but they liked the reflected glory. The jocks enjoyed the attention and were alternately cruel and kind to their worshipers. In the center of it all sat Cummings, his beautiful girlfriend gazing at him adoringly on one side, Vanik smirking and mean on the other.

Coolly appraising them this noon, it struck me that a peculiar relationship existed between the two star athletes. Vanik was smarter, handsomer, and in many ways, just as athletically talented as Cummings. On the field they were a terror to opposing defenses, but in school Vanik seemed only a satellite of Cummings. Maybe it was because people liked Cummings while few could stand Vanik, even his fellow jocks. Perhaps

Vanik knew that without Cummings' friendship, the others would turn away from him, leaving him to float aimlessly in space. God, I knew what that was like.

Suddenly I realized that something about the jock group had changed. Where the hell was Fred? He'd always been there before. Jeff was sitting a couple of places down from me, quiet and sad. "Hey, Jeff. Where's Fred these days?"

Jeff looked over at the jocks disinterestedly. "I don't know. Has he gone somewhere?"

"That's what I'm asking you. I don't think I've seen him in a week, maybe two."

"Maybe that cut Perry gave him got infected or something. God, I hope the son of a bitch dies."

I nodded, sorry I'd even asked Jeff. It just brought everything back for him. A couple of other guys at the table were also looking over in interest. That something had really happened to Fred was almost too much to hope for. I went back to glancing through a history chapter. Fred probably had a cold or something. Not worth worrying about. Let's see—"Wilson and the League of Nations." Do I really care? No, but it'll be on the test.

The day ground down until, with the usual laughing and yelling, the kids flung out the doors for the weekend. Dad and I had a quiet supper, the mood still too strained from the night before to allow much talk. I certainly didn't want to study on a Friday night, but I'd be damned if I was going to ask him if I could go out or even watch TV. So, when the last dish lay drying in the rack, I went to my room and sat at my desk. I calculated the hours left in the school year, then dragged out the damn algebra and turned to my place.

The radio news had just come on at nine o'clock when I heard shattering glass and metallic thumps from below my window. I jumped up and pulled back the drapes. Four kids were smashing at the Buick with two-by-fours and hammers. I guess they saw me, because they ran then. I couldn't recognize any of them in the dark. I heard Dad on the stairs and then he was out front running after them. Not twenty feet from the door he tripped and fell hard. I dropped the drapes and rushed for the stairs.

When I got to him, he was sitting bent forward, holding his left wrist. I knelt by him. "How bad are you hurt, Dad?" He didn't say anything, just sat there rocking back and forth. That scared me more than anything. Lights were coming on and a couple of neighbor ladies came to the door. "Come on, Dad, you can't stay here."

He didn't say anything, just sat rocking. My God, was he finally coming apart? "Dad, please. You can't do anything here. . . . Dad, you're hurt. Let's go inside and look at your arm." I got my hands under his arms from behind and, with every ounce of my strength, tried to lift him to his feet, praying I wouldn't hurt him. He finally came out of his daze a little and made his legs cooperate.

I led him gently past the wrecked car, very conscious of the curious eyes of the two neighbor ladies. At the door Dad turned and together we looked at the smashed windows, the broken headlights, and the dozens of dents in the hood, fenders, roof, and doors of the Buick. His eyes glistened with tears and I knew it was not the damage to the car or his arm that hurt him so terribly, but something immeasurably greater, a hurt so large that no drug, no words, no effort could diminish it.

A squad car rolled up fifteen minutes later and a patrolman came upstairs. We told him all we knew, which wasn't much. He went to talk to the neighbors, but was back in twenty minutes. None of them had seen anything, so it looked like the kids had gotten away clean. The cop asked if Dad had any suspicions on their identities.

Dad shrugged. "A lot of kids don't like me. I could give you a dozen names. But I can't start accusing kids left and right. Their parents would hang me."

The cop didn't look very happy with the answer. "Well, maybe you ought to think about it and talk to one of the detectives tomorrow. He'll know better how to handle it."

Dad thanked him and he left. A while later another squad car pulled up and two officers got out and shot some pictures, but they didn't come to the apartment.

The rest of the evening we sat in front of the TV. Dad didn't mention any rules or quiz me about my studies. He just sat motionless, his swollen wrist resting on a pillow. Twice I asked him if we should go to the hospital, but he just shook his head without looking at me.

I couldn't think of anything else to say. We were connected by blood and the past, but no real lines of communication. Maybe it was my fault, maybe it was his, but try as I could, even now when I wanted so much to comfort him, I could find no words. So we sat in silence, bruised and fearful in our shared, yet vastly distant loneliness.

In the morning I found Dad sitting at the kitchen table in his T-shirt with a sport shirt across his lap. His left wrist had ballooned in the night to twice its normal size. When he looked up, I was shocked to see how gaunt and gray his face was. "I think my wrist is broken. I can't even get my shirt on."

I went to his closet for a short-sleeved one. I heard him talking on the phone as I came back through the living room. "Yes, last night. The car isn't drivable. I hate to ask you, Dan, but you probably live the closest. . . . Thanks. I'll wait downstairs. . . . Right. Thanks again."

"Do you want me to come, Dad?" I held the shirt for him.

"No. You stay here and do your work. The insurance adjuster will be coming and I might not be back in time." He got the buttons and awkwardly stuffed the shirttails into his pants.

"What do I tell him?"

"There shouldn't be much. He'll have the police report, so just answer any questions he has."

"Okay. Just a second, I'll get your coat."

About ten-thirty the insurance man showed up, shot some more pictures, asked a couple of questions, and left in ten

116

minutes. He didn't look very happy about losing part of his Saturday.

I spent the rest of the morning sweeping up the glass from around and inside the car. They'd done a pretty thorough job. I hadn't even noticed the two slashed tires before and the dents looked even worse in the daylight. Not a single piece of glass had escaped unbroken.

Mattson brought Dad home about noon. They spoke for a couple of minutes, then Dad got out. His coat hung loosely over his left shoulder and his arm was immobilized by a cast. "Hey, Dad, can I sign your cast?" I'd been practicing that line.

He tried to smile. "Sure, you can be the first one." He walked once around the car. "Did the insurance man come?"

"Ya, he said we could have it towed in Monday."

Dad nodded and went upstairs. He was in no mood to talk.

I walked downtown and bought some sheet plastic. Back home, I sealed up the broken windows as well as I could. A gentle rain wouldn't harm anything, but a downpour might be trouble. I couldn't face studying yet, so I took a walk, trying to enjoy the brisk spring breeze and the warm sunlight that found an opening in the clouds every now and then. The melting snowbanks had all but disappeared and the yards in the neighborhood were starting to turn green. Spring had slipped into our town so gently I'd hardly noticed, and for once it really hit me: school was going to end. I might even get into Capstone.

I might, that is, if I passed finals. Suddenly the diminishing number of days seemed all too few. God, there was still a ton to do. I might be caught up as far as the current units went, but immense gaps still waited to be filled from last quarter. I'd have to know about numerous chapters I hadn't even glanced at yet.

As I walked home, my brain rapidly ran down my subjects: English—quite a bit there, at least a hundred pages in the text and two novels, not to speak of grammar (God, I hated grammar.); history—a half-dozen chapters at least; speech—there was that handbook on argumentation and debate I hadn't even opened; auto mechanics and phys ed were okay—oh, hell, there was that first-aid workbook I'd barely started. And, of course, there was always the damned algebra. How could I have been so cocky recently? My tail was still very much in hot water. Algebra first. I'd ask Dad for some help. It'd take his mind off his arm and the car.

But the door to the apartment was locked. Inside, a note lay on the kitchen table: "Went out for a while. Don't hold dinner for me. Stick to the homework. Dad."

I rubbed my eyes and glanced at the clock. Nearly eleven o'clock. The novel *Lord of the Flies* was pretty good, and the evening had gone by quickly. But I was worried about Dad. Where could he have gone? I laid the book on my bed and walked to the kitchen for a snack. Halfway there, I heard a fumbling at the door. Dad was apparently having trouble finding the door key. Had the hall light burned out again?

He almost fell in on me when I opened the door. He'd been leaning his left shoulder against it while trying to work the lock. Behind him the hall light burned brightly. "Dad, are you okay?"

He straightened and cleared his throat, gazing at me with bleary eyes. "Ya, ya. I'm okay." His words were slurred with liquor. In shock, I watched him weave his way into the living room. I'd never seen Dad drunk! What should I do? Nothing, probably. He'd be okay. I went to the refrigerator.

There was a crash and a heavy thud in the living room. I ran to the door. He lay on his stomach in the far corner of the room, his shoulders heaving. The table had fallen against the wall, smashing lamp, lamp shade, and bulb. The picture of Mom and Roxy lay facedown next to Dad, its shattered glass strewn across the carpet.

I heard myself say, "Oh, my God!" I went to him and knelt down, putting my arms around him. He was sobbing almost soundlessly, just great gasping breaths of air sucking in and gushing out. "Dad, Dad, it's okay. You fell. It's okay. Everything's okay."

118

We stayed in that awkward position for I don't know how many minutes. Finally, he seemed to quiet. I was afraid he might be falling asleep. I couldn't leave him there. He'd cut himself on all the shattered glass. Worse, what horror to wake amid the ruins of his shrine. For the second time in two days I boosted my father to his feet. "Come on, Dad. You'll feel a lot better in the morning."

In the bedroom he let me undress him almost like a child. I helped him roll between the covers. I wanted to say something, but what? Would he even remember? I went to the door and flipped off the light. "Good night, Dad," I whispered.

"Steven, stay a minute."

I waited for him to speak, then went to his chair and sat in the dark. He seemed to be having a lot of trouble forming his words. "Maybe it'd be better if you slept now, Dad."

He shook his head violently. "Steven, I'm so sorry."

"It's okay, Dad. You just fell."

"I don't mean just tonight. I mean about everything."

"It's okay, Dad," I said softly.

"I wish it was. God, how I wish it was!"

"It will be, Dad. Everything will be fine."

He didn't say anything more and after a few minutes he started to snore.

Back in the living room I set the table upright and swept up the glass. The lamp was broken beyond repair and I took it and the broken glass downstairs and around back to the trash cans. Back in the apartment, I replaced the plate of glass with the one from the picture Dad had given me. I tried not to look too closely at the smiling faces in the pictures—the pretty woman in early middle age who'd been my mother and the little girl who'd been my sister once so long ago.

There was no lamp to replace the broken one, so I left the picture sitting alone on the table and went to bed. I lay there looking at the small square of light reflected on the ceiling by the light outside on the deserted street. This year had better get over quick, I thought. I'm not sure how much more either of us can take.

11

Dad was up early on Sunday, ignoring what must have been a brutal hangover. He made no reference to the previous evening. About his only concession was skipping church. Maybe even he couldn't face people just yet. All day he seemed to take particular delight in hounding me about my progress. He even gave me a lecture about the disorganization of my desk, even though schoolwork, not dirty clothes, littered it now. Ya, he was definitely back in form—the eternal Toad.

In school on Monday he came back harder than ever, broken arm and all, riding his classes like a tyrant and patrolling the halls like Darth Vader. I shuddered when I saw him laying down the law to Cummings, Vanik, and a tight-lipped knot of athletes by the bench outside the theater doors—a bench that the administration, in its peculiar but infinite wisdom, had placed off-limits to students in their free time. I kept on walking, but I felt their malicious eyes following me.

The report on the vandalism of our car appeared in Monday afternoon's paper and by Tuesday noon it was the talk of the school. Everyone was trying to guess who'd done it and waiting for the ax to fall, but I avoided giving anyone the chance to ask me about it.

True to his word, Dad had refused to name suspects in a conference with the Phantom and a detective on Monday afternoon. And he was right not to. Greg was the most obvious one, but there were also the kids Dad had flunked at semester, and, of course, Cummings, Vanik, and their crowd held more than one grudge against Dad. There were just too many possibilities. After all, he wasn't called Toad because kids liked him.

Just before auto mechanics I ran into Trish at the home-ec room door. "Hi, Steve." She pulled me aside from the general crush. "I heard about your car. Did your father break his arm chasing them?" I nodded. "Gee, that's a shame. I felt bad when I heard about it."

"Thanks."

"Do you know who did it?"

"No, there are a lot of possibilities. Maybe Demer and some of his friends. Maybe Cummings and some of the jocks."

"I don't think Jim would do that. He's not the type."

"Maybe not, but I wouldn't bet on it. Dad's had a lot of run-ins with the jocks. I told you about the notes we found on the windshield. I'm pretty sure they did that. Fred almost told me so once."

"Well, he couldn't have wrecked your car. Not where he is now."

"Where's that?"

"Didn't you hear? He's at the clinic down in Springstead."

"Why? What's the matter with him?"

"No one seems to know. A couple of kids said he just started crying in the locker room one day. I guess Mr. Lindon got him into the office and later took him home. Fred hasn't been in school since."

"Wow! I didn't think that guy was even a human being, just an ape."

"I guess everybody's got problems."

"Ya, I guess."

"How'd your dad take the car getting wrecked?"

"Pretty hard." I thought of telling her about him just sitting in the parking lot rocking like some kind of mental patient and then getting drunk the next night and knocking over the shrine. But I couldn't. All that was too private. I couldn't let even her know that much about Dad.

"Well . . . I gotta get to class. I hope things work out okay. Call me tonight, huh?"

"Okay." I walked on. Thank God for Trish. Without her to talk to I'd go crazy.

Cummings dropped in beside me. "You got something going with Big Tits, Wart?"

"No, I ain't got nothin' going with her; she's just a friend." I was surprised at the strength in my voice.

"Boy, I sure would like to get close to them pillows." He nudged me with an elbow, a little too hard to be friendly. I didn't reply. At the turnoff to the shop he put a hand on my arm and turned me to face him. We stood staring at each other. "You know, Wart, you really ought to talk to your old man. He's just coming on a might too strong." His tone was easy, but the hardness in his eyes betrayed him.

For the first time I saw that Cummings was no taller than I was and I could look him right in the eye. "Really? I don't see what concern it is of yours."

"Well," he drawled, reaching out and slowly starting to turn my top shirt button, "I'm going to make it my concern damn quick if the Toad doesn't lay off us."

"Take your damn hand off my shirt!"

Cummings gave the button a vicious twist and it sprang from my shirt and skittered across the hall. My right fist came up as if it had a mind of its own. Cummings slipped the blow expertly and my fist only grazed the back of his head. A shock just below my rib cage nearly lifted me off my feet and sent the wind exploding from my lungs. A second punch slammed against the side of my head, dropping me limp to the floor.

"Here, here! What's going on?" Mr. Hoffman rushed out of his office. Looking up, I could see Cummings through a dull haze in a fighter's crouch, his fists still clenched. His lips were drawn back from his teeth, but not in a smile or a snarl. He looked confused, almost frightened. "You, Cummings, get over there." Hoffman pushed him against a locker. "You other kids, get out of here. Fun's over." The little crowd of onlookers dispersed slowly. He knelt by me. "Are you okay?"

"Ya, I'm okay." I wasn't, far from it. My head swam and I felt like vomiting from the blow to the stomach, but I wasn't going to give anyone the satisfaction of knowing it. I stood up shakily.

"Come on, you two. Up to the office." Hoffman gave us a little push and marched behind us as we walked side by side through the library to the administration wing.

At the door of Mattson's office, Hoffman announced us. "A couple of fighters, Mr. Mattson, no permanent damage."

Mattson looked surprised, then regained his composure. "Thank you, Mr. Hoffman. I'll take care of them. Sit down, gentlemen." Hoffman closed the door.

Mattson looked slowly from one to the other of us. Cummings slumped far down in his chair, studying his knuckles. I sat upright. As bad as I felt, I was going to face this out. I wasn't sure why. I'd just screwed up again, this time royally, but I wasn't going to let my backbone melt any longer.

"So, who started this?" Neither of us spoke. "Well, then," he said impatiently, "who threw the first punch?"

"I did." My voice shook a little bit and I gritted my teeth.

"Were you provoked?"

What a stupid question! Of course I was! I'd been provoked for years. "Yes."

"Well, what was the provocation?" His voice was irritable.

I glanced at Cummings. He hadn't changed position, just slowly worked the fingers of his right hand, his precious passing hand. "Ask him."

"Well, Mr. Cummings?" Cummings just shrugged and slouched deeper in his chair. "Come on, speak up."

"I don't know what caused it. I was just trying to give him some friendly advice."

"Mr. Michaels?"

"That's his side. I didn't see it that way."

Mattson sat staring at us—what a contrast we must have seemed. When he finally spoke, his voice was tired. "Well, you two have to take the prize for stupidity. Cummings, you could lose your eligibility for baseball and walk out of here next year with a black mark on your record—a record, I might add, none too illustrious beyond your ability to propel a football." Cummings shifted uncomfortably. "And you, Michaels, need every minute in school just to pass at the end of the year." It was my turn to lower my eyes. "So I can't see suspending you two, but I'll be damned if I'll let the rules be flouted. I want both of you back here at three-twenty. By that time I'll have come up with something onerous enough to make you sorry for this spectacle."

"I got practice." Cummings' voice was soft, but hard-edged.

For a second I thought Mattson was going to lose his temper, but he came back just as cold. "I don't give a hoot if you've got an appendectomy scheduled, Cummings. You be here or you'll never even swing a ping-pong paddle for this school again. Now get out of here, both of you."

Outside, Cummings stalked away without even looking at me. I stopped long enough to get a hall pass from one of the secretaries, then trudged down to auto mechanics. My stomach was sore and a big lump was swelling on the side of my head, but I could make it.

Mr. Ohm accepted my pass without comment and put me to work changing some tires. Taking off the old tires and putting on the new ones required some hard work, but it wasn't complicated and for once I couldn't lose myself in the work. What was I going to say to Dad? He'd certainly hear about it within the hour. I hadn't been in a fight since grade school, and I'd lost that one badly too. Dad had given me hell for days about fighting then. What would he say now?

The meeting with Mattson at three-twenty was brief. Cummings wore his baseball uniform and carried his well-used glove. I had nothing extra except the bruise on the side of my head and my sore stomach.

"Ah, gentlemen, I've been looking forward to seeing you." Mattson leaned back in his chair, studying us. "I've spoken with the head custodian and he tells me he could use a couple of strapping young fellows to do some heavy work. I'm assigning you each ten hours of work detention starting tomorrow. At an hour and a half or two hours a night, you can be finished by the end of next week. You, Mr. Cummings, are suspended from the baseball team until you complete your detention."

"What about him?" Cummings gestured my way without looking at me.

"He has the same amount of detention."

"Ya, but he doesn't have any practices."

"Well, Mr. Cummings, you want to play baseball and you're suspended from doing that. Mr. Michaels is suspended from doing whatever he wants to do during those ten hours. It strikes me as fair."

"But, I'm starting at short—"

"Mr. Cummings! I can arrange it so you are suspended for the season. Now, you're getting a break, young man. Do you want it or not?"

"Yes, sir," Cummings muttered.

"Do you have any objections, Mr. Michaels? Perhaps you have some brilliant alternatives."

"No, sir."

"Very well, then, you may go. Oh, one more thing. I've instructed the head custodian to assign you jobs where you have to work together. When you've completed your time, I want to hear what you've learned. In detail."

We left. As before, Cummings disappeared down the hall without giving me a glance or saying a word. I would have vastly preferred to flee the building then, delaying the confrontation with Dad as long as possible, but now that he had his arm in a cast, I had to drive him home in the rented car. I went for my books.

He was standing at the demonstration table at the front of the lab, his lips tight, his face white with anger. "Well, I see you didn't run out of the building this time." His voice brimmed with sarcasm.

I dropped my books on a lab table and leaned against it, folding my arms. "Nope."

"Why the hell not? While you're busy destroying my reputation, you might as well make as big a splash as possible."

"I wasn't trying to destroy your reputation."

"Well, you're sure doing a fine job of it for not trying."

I met his blazing eyes. My own temper was building like a tidal wave, but I kept my voice cool. "I'm the one who got hurt, not you."

"Do you really believe that?" I nodded coldly. "Well, then, you're no son of mine." He slammed his good fist against the table. "You can get those withdrawal papers right now. I'll sign them and you can get the hell out of my home tonight. And I'll give you money too—enough to get you just as far away as possible. And I'll give it in your mother's memory, a memory for which you've never had one decent moment of respect."

That did it; the dike of my control broke. "The hell I haven't! I've had as much as you ever did. But don't ask me to leave twice, Dad. I'm finished being your son. It was a lousy job, Dad. A lousy, stinking, rotten, impossible job, and I quit. And here . . ." I took a folder and threw it at him. "Just to prove that the old Wart can make it on his own without any of your goddamn rules." I grabbed my books and plunged for the door. Mr. Ohm stood in my way.

Both Dad and I were momentarily paralyzed by his unexpected presence. He stood looking at us, then turned and quietly closed the door.

"Mr. Ohm," I blurted.

Dad said, "Fritz! I didn't see you there."

He nodded and leaned against a table, studying us. He rubbed his jaw meditatively. "Well, I guess it wasn't my place to hear what I just heard. But I did. And now I guess I'm going to say it: you two better stop yelling at each other and do a little thinking. I don't believe either of you meant what I heard you say. John, you no more want to kick Steve out of the house than I want to go to the moon. And you, Steve, don't want to leave and you don't want to quit." I looked down. Mr. Ohm went on even more quietly. "I don't think you two are in the habit of listening to each other or telling each other the truth. Now, it's probably not my place to say so, but I think you'd better start." He left, closing the door quietly behind him.

I stood with my back to Dad. Neither one of us spoke. I knew we both felt the same thing—absolute, complete humiliation. Mr. Ohm, like a calm lifeguard, had pulled us from the drowning tide of our anger and left us standing drenched and foolish on the desolate beach.

"My God," Dad said, and slumped onto a stool. I dropped my books on the table nearest me and sat on its edge, my back still to Dad. In the reflection of the salamander tank I saw him open the folder I'd thrown at him and slowly page through the contents. "Steve, why didn't you show me these before?"

"Why should I?" I said softly.

"But an A — and three B's . . ."

"And five C's and two D's."

"But the improvement! You should have shown me."

"Why? So you could pick every one apart?"

There was a pause and then he asked quietly, "Is that what you think I would have done?"

I turned to look at him. "Dad, that's what I *know* you would have done. And you should damn well know it too! All my life that's all you've ever done. Get something ninety-eight percent right and you'd go after the other two percent. There's never been any pleasing you. Never, Dad! Not ever!" I turned away again.

"Steve. The fight. What was it about?"

"It doesn't matter."

"Tell me . . . please."

I took a deep breath. "It was about you, Dad. Cummings was threatening you."

He was silent for a long moment. "Steven, I didn't know. You should have told Mr. Mattson."

"You see, Dad, that's what I mean. I can't even defend you without getting criticized. I didn't tell Mattson because I didn't want to drag you into it. For years I've taken crap for you. Can't I even do that well?" My voice was rising again. I slapped my thigh hard.

A long pause followed, then Dad said quietly, "Let's go home and start over, son."

I looked at him. He meant it. I looked down, then nodded. He went to his office for his coat.

On the way to the car he said, "We'll have to thank Fritz, I guess."

I nodded.

The lights were still on in the shop. Mr. Ohm sat at a bench, his big hands carefully, patiently repairing the electric motor on a grinder. A gentle wisp of smoke rose from his old black pipe. He glanced up. "Hi, fellas."

Dad started awkwardly, "Fritz, we wanted to, ah, say thanks and, well, we're sorry you had to see us like that."

"No problem. As long as it did some good."

"I think maybe it did." Dad glanced at me.

I nodded.

A couple of guys came into the shop from the other door. "Mr. Ohm, could we borrow some jumper cables?"

"Sure, boys." He looked at us. "You two have a good evening."

"We will," Dad said.

Perhaps we should have engaged in a long, deep discussion right away, but we didn't. Over supper, we talked about baseball. It took us about two minutes to get in a fight about the Twins. The Twins had made a run for the pennant the previous season and a lot of people thought this might be their year. I didn't think so. A lot of regulars had played way above themselves and the team still hadn't been able to win the worst division in baseball.

Dad disagreed strongly. He'd come up with a theory that saw the Twins blowing away the entire division. He rattled off figures like a computer to prove his case. When I finally got a chance to mention the weak pitching, he dismissed my opinion with a wave of a hand. "Oh, a couple of starters just had off years. They're bound to be better this year and the defense should be stronger too. Now look at the hitting, Steven. They led in the division in doubles, they led in home runs, they led in runs scored. Cripes, look at the figures, Steven, just look at the figures!" Suddenly he stopped and stared at me, then he compressed his lips and looked down, shaking his head. "I do this to you a lot, don't I?"

"Ya, you do, Dad."

"Cripes," he muttered, "can't talk to my own son about something as silly as baseball without sounding like an old-fashioned schoolmaster." He sat staring at the patterned flecks in the Formica tabletop for a long minute, then leaned back and sighed. "I guess that's what I've turned into. I've been teaching a long time, Steven, over twenty years now. Sometimes I think I ought to quit and do something else for a change."

What could I say? Teaching had been Dad's life, but how long could he take the pressure? "Maybe you should, Dad," I said softly.

"But what?" He studied the far corner of the room, his good hand absently massaging the hard surface of his cast. "I don't want to sell insurance or real estate. What else is there for a man my age?"

I didn't have any answers for that. After a couple of minutes, I said, "Dad, let's get the dishes done. I've got studying to do."

He carried the dishes from the table while I washed. He lifted them awkwardly from the rinse water and put them carefully in the drying rack. Although he hadn't complained, I knew how hard it must be for him to teach biology with one arm immobilized. What pleasure it must give those bastards who'd wrecked the car to see him now.

When we were finished, he asked, "Do you need any help tonight?"

"No, I've got things pretty well in hand. I'll call you if I get stuck on the algebra."

"Be glad to help. And, Steven"—he turned to look at me—"let's work on the talking."

What irony that even at the climax of my fight with Dad that afternoon, I'd still grabbed my books before rushing for the door. A few weeks before I would have thrown them all at him, not just the folder containing my few passing exams. The old Wart *had* changed a little bit.

Still, it was nearly impossible for me to study that evening. What a hell of a day it had been. I needed to talk to someone about it—somebody other than Dad. I would have preferred one of the guys, but Keith was long gone and Jeff had been cool to me since Perry's death. So it would have to be Trish—gentle, feminine Trish, who would never understand the kind of anger that had made me take that slow, clumsy, foolish swing at Cummings. She'd listen to my fumbling attempt at explanation, then probably give me hell. But at least she'd listen.

About eight o'clock I went to ask Dad for the car. Perhaps my grounding rules were still in effect, but I thought he'd understand my need to get out for a while. He was sitting in front of the TV, test papers spread out on the coffee table. But he wasn't correcting them. Instead, he had turned and was staring at the picture of Mom and Roxy on the table in the corner. The lamp hadn't been replaced and the photograph sat in shadow. I almost changed my mind about asking for the car. What was in his mind now? What might we end up talking, or more probably yelling, about?

He must have heard me because he turned before I could make up my mind to ask or retreat to my room. "Hello, son. How's it going?"

"Okay, I guess. . . . Dad, I need to get out for a while. I want to talk to Trish, and I mean just talk. Can I have the car? I'll be home in an hour or so."

For a second he hesitated, then nodded. "Okay. The keys are on the hook in the kitchen."

"Thanks, Dad. I won't be long."

I called Trish from the kitchen, hoping fervently that she'd be both willing to go out and able to get permission from her parents. I was lucky.

I guess I'd expected her to ask about the fight right away, but instead she started talking about getting a chance to type on the new computer in business ed. She surprised me by saying she might take a summer-school course to really learn about computers. "I thought you were going to take that camp job again."

"Oh, I might. I haven't made up my mind yet." She said that lightly, but then seemed to brood for a moment before starting to talk about the computer again.

We got hamburgers, fries, and Cokes from the window at Mac's and parked in a corner of the lot.

Trish asked seriously, "So, how are you, Steve?"

"I've been better, I guess."

"I heard about the fight. Did you get hurt bad?"

"I'll live. I've got a hell of a bump on the side of my head, though."

"Let me see." I leaned over and she felt gently. "Ow, that looks like it hurts."

"Ya, it does. I'm probably lucky I didn't get worse. It was pretty stupid to take a swing at him."

"Well, I think all fighting is stupid." She paused and then asked quietly, "Steve, was the fight about me?"

"About you?" I blurted. "Why on earth would you think that?"

She looked away. "Sue Christensen was behind you guys and she told me something he said."

I hesitated. "Ya, well, he did say something."

"About the size of my breasts, right?"

"Ya."

"That jerk!"

I certainly didn't feel like disagreeing with her about Cummings, but I didn't want her to feel bad either. "Well, I don't think he meant much by it, Trish. He was just trying to goad me. I ignored it. I mean, maybe I should have defended you, but—"

"No, I wouldn't ever want you to do that. It's not worth fighting over." She was suddenly on the point of tears and started digging in her purse for a tissue. "Oh, darn! I don't want to cry." She turned away and sat looking out the window, dabbing at her eyes with the tissue.

What was I supposed to say? Trish had always been the one who'd comforted me. "Trish. . . ." I put out a hand to touch her shoulder, but pulled it back. Being touched was probably about the last thing she wanted. "Trish, don't feel bad. It was just a stupid comment. He didn't—"

She interrupted. "Oh, I know guys talk, but why do they have to be so darn crude? I mean, is sex all you guys ever think about?" She turned angry eyes on me.

I squirmed. "Well, it's not what I think about all the time." I shrugged. "I mean, whatever you may think about the way I acted that afternoon in the apartment, I like you for a lot of reasons besides . . . Oh, hell, Trish, what am I supposed to say? Sure guys think a lot about sex, but they think about other things too."

"Twenty or thirty percent of the time," she said bitterly.

"I think that's a little high. Five or ten percent is probably closer."

She couldn't help laughing, and when I thought it was safe, I joined in. In a minute we stopped. She wiped her nose and eyes. "You're funny. . . ." She reached over and squeezed my hand. "I'm sorry I brought that up. I just get paranoid sometimes. Tell me what really happened." I told her about the fight and the meetings with Mattson. "What did your dad say when he found out?"

I grimaced. "The shit really hit the fan." I described the scene and Mr. Ohm's intervention.

When I'd finished, she said, "It sounds to me like maybe something good came out of it, after all. I mean, if you can talk more without getting so mad, maybe it was all worth it."

"Maybe, but I'm not very optimistic. Nothing has ever

helped much in the past. After that big fight we had over you being at the apartment, things were better for a while, but not long. Something is bound to happen and we'll start yelling again."

"Why do you fight so much?"

"It beats me. It's been that way for a couple of years now. We just can't seem to talk about anything without getting in a fight. Maybe we just don't like each other anymore."

"I don't believe that."

"Well, I don't have any other answer."

She paused, then asked very quietly, "Steve, is it something about your mom?"

I lifted my hand and let it drop. "I don't know. He always brings her up when he wants to cut me off. I mean, what he said this afternoon about me not honoring her memory—it was like he'd been practicing that one, saving it up until he really wanted to hurt me."

"But it seems to me he hurts himself just as much." She was silent a moment. "How long has it been, Steve?"

"Three years. Three years a week from next Saturday."

"Three years is a long time."

I sighed. "Ya, I know. But it doesn't seem very long."

"Steve, what are you going to do now? You're not going to start thinking that crazy stuff about dropping out, are you?"

"No. I've gotten this far, I might as well finish the year. After that, I don't know. If I can get into Capstone, things will be okay. But now I've got this damned detention to work off. That's ten hours I can't spare."

"I bet you make it."

"God, I hope so."

"What are you going to do this summer?"

"I don't know. I'd like to get out of this damn town, find a job, and spend the summer away from Dad. I'd just like to be Steve Michaels for a change, not Wart, son of Toad." I sat silent for a moment. Oh, hell, I was sounding sorry for myself again. "How about you? You sound pretty interested in that computer class."

"Not that much, really. I was just too embarrassed to ask about the fight right away. And I guess I have been thinking about it a little, because camp might not be as much fun this year."

Dare I hope? "Why? What's changed?" I asked, trying to sound casual.

"Oh, that guy I met last summer hasn't written in a long time." Her voice caught and she took a deep breath. "I'm not saying it's over, but . . . maybe he's got someone else now." She turned away to look out the window again.

I felt like getting out and dancing on the car hood. Hope! "Well," I said, keeping my tone light, "you've always got me. Just don't expect me to take on any football players for you."

She laughed, brushing away a couple of tears. "Yes, I've always got you, Steve." She reached over to give me a quick hug. "You're a good friend."

I'd like to be a lot more, I thought, but didn't say anything, just laughed too. Maybe in time. With luck!

12

Even if I didn't like it, I was almost becoming used to my notoriety around school. Some of the dirts even considered me something of a hero for taking a swing at Cummings. The smarter ones thought I was just nuts. When I ran into Jeff, he just shook his head and said, "Jeez, are all my friends trying to self-destruct or something? Keith disappears, Perry drives in front of a truck, and now you start trying to beat up Cummings. Are you doing some really heavy dope, man? Because if it ain't drugs, you ought to get your head examined."

"I'm okay. I just hyped out for a second."

"Well, you'd better not do it again, because next time you're going to get stomped until you're about an inch thick. And then they'll get serious."

"Don't worry about it. I'm making it."

"I don't know, man." He walked off shaking his head. After that I saw even less of Jeff.

At least the jocks didn't give me any crap about the fight. When I met a group of them, led as usual by Cummings, they ignored me—even Vanik. I figured Cummings must have given the order not make any reference to the fight. Even though he'd whipped me good and quick, I sensed that he was embarrassed. Imagine the Wart taking a swing at the mighty Jim Cummings. If the dirts were starting to fight back, the jocks must be getting soft.

But I didn't have time to get caught up in the jock/dirt crap again. Finals were less than a month away and I still had to get through a mountain of information. So, I ignored them all—jocks, dirts, and everybody else. I even started bringing a bag lunch and reading in Dad's office while I ate. He'd be either in the teachers' dining room or supervising in the cafeteria during my lunch period. Privacy, that's what I needed now.

After school on Wednesday, Cummings and I started working off our detention. We'd been given the job of painting one of the storerooms in the basement. First we had to move a lot of heavy boxes of old textbooks to another room. We worked pretty well together, unwilling to talk, but naturally anticipating each other's moves. Once Cummings said, "Hey, Wart, get that box next," and I snapped, "The name's Steve, Cummings, not Wart." His eyes blazed and I thought he was going to hit me again, but he just heaved another box on his shoulder and lugged it out.

Thursday afternoon I had auto mechanics. Midway through the second hour Mr. Ohm called me away from balancing a wheel and led the way to his office. "Have a chair, Steve." He sat behind his desk. "Things okay?"

"Ya, okay."

"Good." To my surprise he didn't ask anything about my life at home or in school. "I got a letter yesterday from an old friend who used to be vocational-arts chairman at my first high school. For years he's worked during the summer as director of Broken Arrow Camp outside Minocqua. Do you know where Minocqua is?"

"Ya, Dad and I went fishing near there once."

"Good country for fishing. Anyway, every summer Pete's been hiring a camp mechanic from his high school's Capstone class. But he retired last year and now he's had some kind of hassle with the new vocational-arts chairman. So, he wants me to send a student instead. Would you be interested?"

Answered prayers! "You bet!"

"Now don't be too quick. The job doesn't pay much, and if

there isn't any work to do on the vehicles, you'll be expected to work on the buildings and so on."

My mind was a jumble of thoughts. I'd be away from Brandt Mills and Dad. I'd have a job I'd enjoy. *And* I wouldn't be far away from where Trish worked—if she took the job again. "I wouldn't mind that, Mr. Ohm. I mean, as long as it's not sixteen hours a day or something."

He laughed. "No, Pete's a fair man and you'd learn a lot from him too. If you ran into anything you couldn't handle, he'd be happy to help. He's a fine mechanic. But there's one catch."

"What's that?"

"You'll have to be signed up for Capstone. Pete was one of the founders of the program and he made it very clear that he wants a Capstone student. Now, normally I'd recommend a guy who'd been in the program a year, but I know you can handle the work. Still, you'll have to be enrolled for next year. Otherwise, I'll have to give the chance to somebody else."

I nodded. Wow, I just had to make that C average. "My grades are coming up a little. I think I may make it yet."

"Good. I'll depend on you. Of course, your dad will have to approve too."

"I'll talk to him tonight."

"Fine. Let me know as soon as you can."

Working with Cummings in the storeroom after school, I was so excited I could hardly keep from babbling to him about it. But, hell, he wouldn't care. He wasn't exactly concerned with my good fortune. So, we worked in silence again.

Some of my excitement drained away on the drive home with Dad. How was I going to approach him about it? I could think of a dozen reasons he might object. Since the big fight we'd both been trying very hard to get along, but this could easily turn into another argument.

At supper I explained it carefully. For once he listened without interrupting. When I finished, he said slowly, "Well, Steven, I don't know. You're pretty young yet."

I'd been expecting that one. "I know, Dad, but Mr. Ohm thinks I can do the job, and a summer away might be just what I need."

"You've never been away from home for more than a week."

"But I've got to start sometime, Dad."

"True, but the work will be an awful lot of responsibility for a sixteen-year-old boy."

"I'll work my tail off, Dad. Haven't I proved I can in the last few weeks?"

He nodded and sat silent. After a minute, he pushed back his plate and stood up. "Let me think about it." He walked into the living room.

Damn. Was he just figuring out the best way to say no? I busied myself cleaning up the dishes. Even the smallest good impression might help now. Glancing into the next room, I saw him standing in front of the picture of Mom and Roxy, slowly massaging his arm above the cast.

I was half through with the dishes when he came back into the kitchen. "Okay, Steven. I'll have to admit I'm a little skeptical, but since Fritz thinks it'll work out, I'll go along with it."

I could hardly contain myself and almost dropped a plate. "Great, Dad! You won't regret it, I promise."

I worked all the harder that night. Several times I almost called Trish. I desperately wanted to tell her about it, but I hesitated. She might not be going back at all, and even if she was, would she want me within fifty miles? After all, we really didn't have anything going other than my fantasies. And there was her damn boyfriend too. If he reappeared, I'd really be out of luck.

When I couldn't concentrate anymore, I went to the kitchen and dialed. I'd just tell her about the job and not mention I'd be nearby.

She brought it up herself. "Broken Arrow Camp! I know where that is. It's only about five miles from the camp where I work. We could even see each other once in a while."

"That would be fun," I said. (And how!) "So you've decided to go back?"

"Maybe. I'm not sure. Depends if something better comes up."

"Well, I hope you go back. I'd like to see you. Uh, hey, I'd better get back to work now. Got an English test tomorrow."

"Okay. Do good. I'll see you in school."

I was humming on the way back to my room. Dad glanced up from his chair, his eyebrows raised. "Just feeling good," I said, and grinned.

Back at my desk, I thought, Okay, Wart, settle down. A lot can still go wrong. Do the English first. Then algebra. Damn that algebra. And her boyfriend. I hope something big and heavy got dropped on him. Just heavy enough to keep him in a coma for a decade or so. Like a safe or something.

Friday afternoon after all the other kids had left for the weekend, Cummings and I washed the walls of the storeroom so the paint would stick. It was nearly quitting time when Cummings hurled a rag to the floor and swung to face me. "Damn it, Wart, what made you do a damn fool thing like that?"

"Like what?"

"Like taking a poke at me."

"What's the matter, you God or something?"

"You're pretty cocky for such a wimp."

"So I wasn't born a jock. Am I supposed to commit suicide or something?"

"You damn near did! I could really have cleaned up on you."

"So why didn't you?" We stood glaring at each other.

He turned away tight-lipped, reached in the pail for another rag, crushed the water out of it angrily, and went back to scrubbing the wall. I continued on my section of wall and for several minutes there was no sound except the wet rags on the concrete.

At last he stopped. "I was too damn surprised, that's why.

What the hell business does somebody like you have taking a punch at somebody like me?"

That made me mad, but when I looked in his eyes, I saw genuine confusion there. Cummings' whole world view had been upset by my sudden swing. After all, what *had* someone like me been doing taking a swing at someone like him? It *had* been suicidal. The whole thing still confused me, too. Finally, I said quietly, "You just pushed me too far."

Cummings grunted and we went back to work. A half-hour later we finished for the day, locked the door, and went our separate ways.

Except for church on Sunday, I worked almost all weekend. Every now and then a voice in the back of my mind would say, "You can't make it, Wart. Why get your hopes up? It'll just be worse when you fail. What's all this crap about Capstone and a summer job and Trish anyway? Don't kid yourself, Wart. It ain't going to happen."

But I throttled my self-doubts and told that voice to get screwed. I just had to believe I could make it. Damn it, I would make it! If I could just keep pushing . . .

In the middle of Saturday afternoon I was fighting my way through a chapter in my history text—"Changing American Customs and Life-styles." God, how boring. I pushed the book away and sat with my eyes closed. Rest a minute. "Changing American Customs and Life-styles"—dull, dull, dull. Childbirth . . . christening . . . schooling . . . games and sports . . . courtship (barn dances, hope chests, and dowries, for God's sake) . . . weddings . . . married life . . . child-rearing . . . care of the aging . . . death . . . funerals . . .

I glanced sharply at the picture of Mom and Roxy on my dresser. I'd almost forgotten; a week from today was the anniversary. Next Saturday, Dad and I would stand by their graves and mourn again for them and what might have been. I gazed for a long time at the two smiling faces. So long ago now. Someday we'd have to put away all that might have been—should have been—but wasn't.

I got up and opened a dresser drawer. Then after a moment, I closed it. No, not there. I took the picture to the far dim corner of my room and put it on the bookcase. There. Now I could look at it when I wanted to, not every time I glanced up from my studies. I returned to my desk and turned a page in the history book.

The first three days at school the next week were quiet. Old lady Rawls handed back our English tests: C+, not bad. In speech we gave reports on famous speeches from history. The toughest part was delivering part of the speech in dramatic fashion. I didn't feel much like John F. Kennedy when I read part of his inaugural address, but I did well enough to get a C, although I'd hoped for better.

Cummings and I didn't work Monday afternoon because he had a dentist's appointment. (Super Jock with cavities!) On Tuesday we worked as before, exchanging words only as necessary. But we were getting used to each other.

We finished painting the storeroom Wednesday afternoon about five-thirty. Actually, our detention had been up at four-thirty, but by unspoken agreement we finished the last wall anyway. As I started to clean up the brushes, Cummings stood back and surveyed the avocado-green walls. "God, what an ugly color!" It was the first conversational statement he'd made. I laughed. "Where do you suppose they get this crap?" he asked.

"I don't know. Maybe it's army surplus."

He came over and lent a hand with the brushes. "I guess we gotta see Mattson tomorrow."

"I guess so."

"Do you have ten minutes free just before one?" I nodded. "Let's get it done then. I want to make practice, and besides, that'll only give him a few minutes to chew on us."

"Sounds good to me."

We parted at the outside door by the gym after returning the storeroom key to the janitor on duty. Cummings called, "See you about ten to one."

"I'll be there."

"Good enough. Take care."

The friendly words caught me by surprise. "Ya, you too," I said to his retreating back.

At twelve-fifty the next afternoon I met Cummings coming up from the cafeteria. "Hi ya, Wart. I'm not looking forward to this."

I let the name go. "No, neither am I."

We passed through the main office and Cummings knocked lightly on Mattson's half-open door. "Mr. Mattson, we've put in our ten hours and finished painting the room."

Mattson looked up from some papers on his desk. He looked distracted and tired. A few beads of sweat dotted his forehead despite the coolness of the room. "Oh, yes. Come in, boys. Sit down. Did you learn anything working together?"

Cummings looked down. "Well, I guess we work pretty well together."

"Anything else?"

Cummings shifted uncomfortably and glanced quickly my way. "I don't know. Nothing much really."

Mattson half-stood, his hands violently bunching the papers on his desk. For a moment his mouth worked, then he gave a terrible, wordless yell and pitched forward across the corner of his desk, carrying with him the ashtray, metal baskets, and what seemed like reams of paper.

I don't remember thinking in those first seconds. I don't even remember leaving my chair. I was down beside him, turning him faceup. "My God, I think he's had a heart attack," I said. I felt desperately for a pulse, but couldn't find any. Cummings was yelling for help. I jerked open Mattson's mouth and gave him four quick breaths like they'd taught us as freshmen in health. I checked for the pulse again. Nothing. Cummings was still yelling. I grabbed his arm. "Have you had CPR?" He nodded dumbly. "Then start resuscitation."

Cummings grabbed Mattson's face by the forehead and jaw and began blowing air into his lungs while I started the chest compressions. God, health classes had been so long ago! Could I remember everything right? Beneath my hands, the bones of Mattson's rib cage moved in and out and I found myself counting mechanically out loud, "One one thousand, two one thousand . . ."

"He's breathing," Cummings shouted.

I leaned back, watching the breath suck in through the blanched, drooling mouth. For the first time I heard excited voices. "The ambulance is on the way," someone yelled.

Cummings vomited noisily in the wastebasket. Mattson let out a long, slow breath, and stopped. Cummings heaved again in the wastebasket.

"Jim, for God's sake, get his heart. He's stopped breathing again."

I grabbed Mattson's head and clamped my mouth over his. His lips were lax and slippery, his mustache wet with drool. I blew in hard and fast, pulling the wind in through my nose and pushing it into his lungs. In the distance I could hear Cummings counting in a choked voice. For what seemed like an hour, but was probably only five or six minutes, we continued, then a big hand closed on my shoulder and pulled me away. "I've got it, son."

It was Mr. Lindon. On the other side Mr. Yelle, another of the gym teachers, was pushing Cummings aside. They were CPR instructors and we didn't argue, just stood back.

By the time the ambulance arrived, the crush of adults had pushed us out the door and into the main office. The paramedics rushed in with a stretcher. Ten minutes later, they wheeled Mattson out. They had a tube in his arm and tubes running over his beard to his nose. Mattson looked like a cadaver, but I could see he was still breathing. Mr. Lindon stood near us.

"How is he?" I asked.

"Huh? I don't know. He stopped breathing twice on us in there." For the first time he seemed to recognize us. "Say, you're the two who got to him first, aren't you?"

"Yes."

"Good thinking, boys." He shook our hands. "You may have saved his life. Excuse me. I've got to talk to the boss."

We stood around as things slowly settled down. The Phantom came over and shook our hands. He knew Cummings, of course, but had to ask my name. "Oh, John's boy." I nodded. "You did a good turn, boys. Mr. Lindon tells me you did just right."

"I hope so," I said.

He slapped Cummings on the shoulder with forced good humor. "Football hero and now first-aid wonder."

Cummings shook his head, looking down at his shoes. "Wart here did most of the work."

"Wart?"

"Ya, that's what we call Steve." Cummings took a deep breath and looked up. "If there's any credit, he should get it. I just got sick."

"That's not true," I protested. "You did as much as I did. Besides, what difference does it make?"

The Phantom smiled a little uncertainly. "Well, I think you both did fine. Not too many young men your age could have done as well. Now, why don't you both go relax? Take a stroll. It's a beautiful day." He marched off acting very much in charge and I wondered if he'd remember me in ten minutes. Not likely. We got our coats and headed outside.

We walked across the parking lot and out past the football field, avoiding the soggy spots in the grass. The May sun fell hot on our backs and I unbuttoned my jacket. Cummings walked with his head down, not speaking. Finally, I said, "Jim, for God's sake, what's eating you? You did fine. Mattson's alive. That's all that counts."

"I shouldn't have gotten sick," he muttered.

"So what? I felt like it too. I just didn't get around to it."

"But, damn it, you were cooler in there than I was. And that bothers me." He turned to me, his voice rising. "I'm supposed to be the leader, but there you were giving all the orders while I was puking my guts out." His eyes were blazing. We stared at each other for long seconds, then the fire seemed to die in him.

"I just should have done better," he said softly. "I know that shouldn't be important to me now, but it is."

We walked on, kicking through an uncut field as we got farther from the school. I felt a strange mix of depression and euphoria. Depression because right now Mattson might be dead despite all anyone could do. Euphoria because I'd met a huge and unexpected crisis with enough control to get through. I knew that part of my reaction was selfish, as selfish as Cummings' terrible criticism of himself, but I couldn't help feeling a little proud of myself.

Cummings' usual sunny confidence had disappeared, leaving his face dark and brooding. I felt sorry for him. I didn't have to live up to anyone's image of the hero. In a way I was a lot freer than Cummings. Finally, I said carefully, "Being in control means a lot to you, doesn't it?"

"Ya, a lot. It's all I want in life—to be able to face situations others can't. I love being a quarterback, to run an offense, to control the game."

"Well, you've got that."

"You think so? Hell, they'll probably make me into a defensive back in college. I throw a football pretty good, but a lot of other guys do it better. You should see that guy Peters from Ashland. Hell, he's light-years ahead of me. There are an awful lot of good high-school quarterbacks. I'm not really big enough to compete with most of them."

"So what are you going to do?"

"Oh, I'll take a scholarship, but I'm going to join ROTC too. I'll never be a pro athlete, but I can be an army officer. That'll give me most of what I want. I guess that sounds pretty arrogant, doesn't it? Always wanting to boss other people around."

"You do it well. There's nothing wrong with wanting to be in charge. Somebody's got to do it."

He turned his head and studied me for a long moment. "You know, Wart, you are one hell of a lot smarter than I thought you were. And not a bad guy either. I'm glad I got to know you better."

I felt embarrassed and complimented too. In a way I'd always looked up to Cummings, even when I'd hated him most. "Well, thanks. I'm glad I've gotten to know you too. I wish you'd use my real name, though."

He laughed and slapped me on the back. "I'm sorry. I'll try to remember. Hell, I didn't even know your real name until the other day." We turned back for the school. "How about you, Steve? Going to be a teacher like your old man?"

I glanced at him sharply, but there was no ironic smile on his lips. How little he really knew about me. "No, I'm not cut out for that. I like cars. I want to get into Capstone and find a job as a mechanic after graduation."

"Hmmm . . . well, it's what makes you happy, I guess. I don't like fixing things. I like everything new and running smooth. When I start a car, I want to twist the key and hear that sucker roar."

I laughed. "Well, then you've got to have guys like me to tune the engine now and then."

"I suppose so. But, hey, what do your folks think of you becoming a mechanic? I mean, I'd think the Toad, ah, your dad, would want you to go to college."

"Well, he did. Probably still does, but we've kind of worked that out. My mom's dead."

"Oh, I didn't know. When did that happen?"

"Three years ago. She and my sister were killed in a car accident."

We walked in silence for a minute. "That was a year before we moved to town. I'm sorry, Steve. I didn't know."

"It's okay. No big deal now."

"Is that why your old man is always in a lousy mood?"

That caught me off guard. Cripes, Cummings was no fool. "Part of it, maybe. There are other things, too. Like me."

"You don't get along?"

"Not too good."

He nodded. After a minute he let out a deep breath and said, "Hey, I'm sorry about last week, Steve. I guess that was my fault. But why the hell has your old man got it in for me

146

and the guys? I mean, you talk about pushing too far! Hell, I almost had to tackle Vanik to keep him from going after the Toad that morning."

Maybe he'd just forgotten, but using that name again made me mad. "You guys are pretty good at pushing people too."

He stopped and looked at me hard. "Maybe."

"Maybe, hell! You know damn well you are. This jock/dirt thing got one guy killed this year."

He grimaced. "Ya, and almost put another in the nuthouse."

"Fred?" He nodded. "Is it that bad?"

"It ain't good, I hear. He's staying with his aunt and uncle down in Springstead and seeing a shrink two or three times a week."

"I'm surprised the doctor can find anything to work on."

Cummings looked at me quizzically, then snorted and shook his head. "Ya, Fred's a beauty, ain't he? About as much common sense as a blocking dummy . . . and your buddy didn't have much more." He started walking again and I followed along. "I've felt bad about the whole thing, but what can anyone do?"

"Everybody could knock off this jock/dirt crap."

"Maybe, but that's damn easy to say and pretty tough to do. You may think I'm the leader of the jocks and I guess in a way I am, but I'm not a dictator."

"You could do something."

"Ya, I've been thinking about that. Especially since you and I got into it last week. With Fred and Perry I just figured it was two stupid guys and lousy luck. But you and me? That was a little different."

"Well, why did you start it anyway?"

He shrugged. "In part because I was really pissed at your old man. That was a close call with Vanik that morning. I mean, Tom's my friend and a hell of a fine football player, but you've got to be careful with a guy like him, even if you're a teacher. He's got a mean streak as wide as a four-lane highway. I know that and I even like it because when I hand him

147

the ball he's going to get yardage just because he likes hitting people. Off the field I can keep him cool most of the time. But, I tell you, that was real close last week."

"I don't think I know what happened."

"We were playing volleyball in gym and Tom set up a ball for a spike and this other kid blew it. It cost Tom's team the game and, boy, does he hate to lose. He damn near castrated that kid. Lindon heard him yelling and got Tom aside after class and really reamed him. Tom thinks Lindon's just about God, so he was really in a bad mood when we got to the cafeteria a couple of minutes late. And there was your dad. He gave us some crap about obeying the rules and sent us back to get a pass from Lindon. Hell, it'd only been a couple of minutes and we had to waste another ten finding Lindon and getting a lousy pass. We came back and I gave your dad the pass, but instead of letting us go, he started laying more crap on us. He repeated everything he'd said before and then went on and on about how athletes should set a good example. Hell, I don't remember it all. Anyway, I just saw Tom's eyes start to change. I've seen it in a ball game when he's been stopped for a loss. It's like he doesn't see anybody around him anymore; he's all inside himself. I don't know what he finds there and I'm not sure I want to know, but next time he gets the ball, watch out. He'll kill somebody for a yard."

"Why do you like him?" I asked quietly, hardly believing I could talk this way to Cummings.

He shrugged. "Because he does what he has to do to win. And if you want to be a winning quarterback, you need people like him."

"Well, why do you have to win all the time? If it takes that, I'm not sure it's worth it."

He stopped and turned to face me. "Look, Steve, I don't want to get into all that. Maybe winning isn't what you need, but it's what I need. Now I'm just trying to tell you that your old man has got to cool it. If I hadn't been there, I think Tom would have blown. I apologized to your dad real quick and that settled things down. But having to do that pissed me off.

Maybe we'd been a couple of minutes late, but we didn't deserve all that crap. One of these days your old man is going to push too hard and there's going to be real trouble. No shit, Steve, bad trouble."

We started walking again. After a couple of minutes I asked softly, "Like with the car?"

"Huh? Oh, ya, I heard about that. Pretty bad?"

"Over fifteen hundred dollars. The insurance covered everything except the hundred-dollar deductible, but the car will never really be the same."

"Well, whatever you or your dad think, it wasn't Vanik or me or any of our crowd. That's not our style."

"But one of you put the notes on our windshield."

He nodded. "Ya, that was Tom's idea and it wasn't a good one, but I don't think anybody thought we'd really do something. And we didn't. Do you believe me?"

"Yes."

"Good." He brooded for a long minute, then said slowly, "There's just been too much crap going on this year. I guess I'm going to try to stop some of it." We were almost back to the parking lot now and we paused, both unwilling to enter the school quite yet. "You know," he said, "we sure have been talking a lot about other things and not much about Mattson."

"Ya, I know. I thought of that too."

"Well, I hope he lives. He ain't exactly one of my favorite people, but . . ."

"I know."

"Still, it's funny that we've talked about ourselves so much. It's kind of like you never really know someone until you're in a tight spot with him. Then I guess you can talk." I nodded. "Well, I suppose we've got to go back into that damn school." He led the way.

Near the door I had to ask, "Jim, do you know who wrecked Dad's car?"

He didn't answer right away, but finally he said, "Ya, I know."

"Who?"

"Do you really want to know? You couldn't prove anything. Neither could I. It would just cause a lot of trouble."

"I'd still like to know."

He paused and thought. "Well, I guess I'm not going to tell you. No way would it solve anything. But I'll get the hundred bucks for you."

"I think it'd be better if we just gave the names to the police."

He shook his head and his eyes were hard again. "No, we do this my way or not at all. If you tell your old man or the Phantom that I know who did it, I'll just deny it. My way or no way." I shrugged, a little hurt at his harshness after our friendship of the last half-hour. He softened. "Take care, Steve. You won't have any more trouble with Vanik and the guys. Leave that to me. And I'll try to get them off your dad, too, but keep him cool."

"He doesn't listen to me, Jim."

He stood chewing his lip for a second. "I guess that's a problem a lot of us have with our folks. Well, I'll see you." He swung in through the door.

I'd missed history and most of study hall, and, of course, speech would be canceled. So, I went to the library and sat out the rest of the day. The kids were already buzzing about the incident, but I ignored it and tried to read an English assignment.

When Dad came down to his room from the teachers' lounge, his face was grim.

In the Buick I asked, "Did you hear anything?"

"I guess he's alive, but it doesn't sound good." We rode in silence for a couple of blocks. "I heard you were there."

"Ya, Jim Cummings and I gave a hand."

"I heard it was more than that."

I told him all about it then, surprised at how much I wanted to play back every detail. Dad listened in silence. I'd had the car parked for two or three minutes before I finished.

150

He sighed. "Well, son, whatever happens, you did as well as you could. I'm proud of you."

"I just did what anyone else would have done. No big deal."

He looked at me searchingly. "No, Steven, I don't think most people would have done what you did. It was a big deal. You've got a lot more steel in you than I thought. I don't know where on earth you got it, but I'm beginning to see it, even if you haven't." He paused and we looked at each other curiously. Then he said very softly, "It probably came from your mother."

"Maybe it came from you, Dad."

We sat in silence. A few drops of rain hit the windshield. Dad slapped his good hand on my knee. "It's starting to rain. Come on, let's get something to eat."

Friday I was struck by how quickly people resumed their normal lives. After Perry's death in the winter, things had been a lot quieter. But it was spring now and there were a lot more things to think about. A few kids asked me what I'd had to do with everything, but I put them off and went about my business.

The afternoon paper carried a story on page three about it. Cummings and I were mentioned as having given first aid on the scene. Mattson was in critical but stable condition. I cut out the paragraph about us and taped it above my desk. Except for marriage and death, I thought, I'll probably never make the paper again. I might as well enjoy it.

13

I walked downtown Saturday morning, my algebra book and folder under my arm. The weather didn't match my mood. I would have preferred a dark, gloomy day with a little rain and a chill wind. Instead, the sun shone hot in a bright, cloudless sky. People were outside in their warm-weather clothes working on their lawns, starting gardens, washing cars and playing catch. Summer was here if only for the day, and everyone was enjoying it. But I had the afternoon and the anniversary visit to the cemetery to get through and I wished the weather was crummy and everyone as miserable as I was.

I'd slept poorly, bad dreams waking me twice. For once I'd been up before Dad. I'd stood outside in the morning chill, watching the sun rise over the tall stacks of the mill. Three years ago today, I thought. Sometimes it seemed like three days, sometimes like a million years.

Dad had left around eight-thirty to go into school, saying on his way out that we'd go up to the cemetery after lunch. I'd tried studying, but couldn't concentrate in the confines of the apartment. I'd headed downtown with the idea of studying at the library, but as I got close, I just kept on walking. Studying was out of the question; the past hung about me too closely today.

Mom and Roxy had been killed early on a Wednesday evening a hundred miles from home. About nine o'clock Dad had just told me to get ready for bed when the doorbell rang. A thin, gray-haired man in a gray coat stood hat in hand. Behind him loomed a big, uniformed cop. "Mr. Michaels, I'm Lt. Eckler and this is Officer Michalek. We'd like to see you for a few minutes on a personal matter."

"Yes, of course. Come in." Dad turned to me, his face white. "Steven, go to your room now."

"What do they want, Dad?"

"Never mind. Just go to your room."

I went upstairs and knelt on the landing in the dark. I could see part of the living room from there and hear their voices. The gray man was speaking. "I'm afraid we have some bad news, Mr. Michaels. Perhaps if we could sit down . . ."

"Yes, of course. Please."

They all sat. I could see the two policemen, but not Dad. The gray man reached inside his coat and took out a sheet of yellow paper. "We received this teletype message from state police headquarters at seven-forty. The message says that your wife and daughter were involved in an automobile accident about five-fifteen this afternoon on the U.S. Fifty-three exit off I-Ninety-four south of Eau Claire." I heard Dad gasp. The gray man looked down at the carpet. The big uniformed cop shifted nervously in his chair. "We're very sorry, Mr. Michaels. They were taken to Sacred Heart Hospital in Eau Claire, but nothing could be done. They were dead on arrival."

"There must be some mistake." Dad's voice was desperate.

"I'm terribly sorry, sir, but we are very careful in these cases." I could hear Dad start sobbing quietly. The gray man went on, "Now, we would be glad to help you contact other family members, your minister, or a funeral director. Whatever we can do to help."

I knelt there watching the two policemen and listening to Dad cry. This must be some kind of game, a horrible, cruel game, but a game. Thirteen-year-old boys didn't lose their mothers and sisters. In a minute the gray man would tell Dad that it had all been a game and everything would be all right again.

"My son," Dad choked out, "I can't tell him now. Somebody to stay with him."

"Yes, of course. Who would you like us to call?"

"I don't . . . The kids have a baby-sitter. Mrs. Timmons. She's an older woman."

"Dorothy? Yes, she baby-sits for my children too." Children? He couldn't have any kids. I couldn't imagine the gray man as a father. "Jim, will you call her, please? Dorothy Timmons."

The big cop got up and walked toward the kitchen. He glanced up and I pulled back quickly. I heard him pause, then turn back to the living room. He'd seen me. I ran into my bedroom and stood in the dark facing the door. There were muffled noises below and then Dad's hurried step on the stairs. He came in. His face was ashen and tearstained, but he tried to smile. "Time for bed, Steven. Let's hurry."

"Dad, what's going on?"

"It's okay, Steven." He pulled back the covers. "Quick now, it's late."

"But, Dad . . ."

"It's all right. Please get in bed, now. Don't worry, everything is going to be fine."

Unwillingly, I started getting into my pajamas. "But he said . . ."

"Yes, there's been an accident, but don't worry about . . ." He had to take a deep breath. "Don't worry about your mother and sister. We'll talk in the morning. Mrs. Timmons will be here for a while. Ready?"

I got in bed. "Dad . . ."

"It's okay, Steven. Everything will be fine in the morning." He covered me up and bent down to kiss me on the forehead. "Go to sleep, son. I'll be near."

But he wasn't. The police stayed until Mrs. Timmons came. I heard her voice in the distance. "Oh, Mr. Michaels . . ." And then Dad left with the gray man and the big cop. Left me alone in the dark trying to tell myself that everything was okay, that the morning would be like other mornings.

I slept, and the policeman took Dad to Mr. Ohm's. Dad and Mr. Ohm drove the hundred miles to Eau Claire and weren't back until long after Mrs. Timmons had made me breakfast and told me I didn't have to go to school that day. I knew that, and I knew a lot of other things. But everyone treated me like a child and no one told me the things I didn't know or couldn't understand.

I sat all morning with Mrs. Timmons on the couch in front of the TV. A few times the phone rang, but she told people to call back later. When I tried to talk to her, she said to be patient until Dad got home. So we just sat watching dumb quiz shows. I tried to lose myself in them, tried to ignore what down deep I knew was the truth: Mom and Roxy were dead. I tried so hard that once I actually forgot and laughed at a quiz master's stupid joke. Mrs. Timmons gave me a startled, horrified look, then turned quickly back to watching the show. After that I sat silent. That look had said enough—it really had happened.

When Dad and Mr. Ohm came in about eleven o'clock, Mrs. Timmons went to the kitchen to make coffee. Dad came into the living room and sat by me. He pushed his glasses up on his forehead and rubbed his eyes. "Steven, your mother and sister are . . . gone."

I watched the TV —*The Price Is Right*. Lots of happy people winning wonderful things. "I know."

"Steven, nothing could be done —"

I started crying and he wrapped his arms around me. "I'm here, Steven. I'll always be here. We've got to be brave."

"I don't want to be brave," I choked.

"I know. I know. Neither do I, but we have to be."

"Why didn't you take me with you? Why did you leave me alone?"

"Steven, . . . I . . . I just . . . hoped that there was some mistake, some chance. Please, son, try to be brave. We'll get through this somehow."

We sat that way for a long time, both crying. Me loud, him quiet. In the background I could hear the TV show—the laughter, the applause, the whoops of the winners.

By midafternoon the house started to fill up. Dad's brother and his wife and four kids arrived from Minneapolis. My Aunt Mary took charge while Dad and Uncle Jerry went to see the funeral director. In the late afternoon and on into the evening people came to call. They were good people and they meant well, but I was angry with them. They couldn't understand. They couldn't make anything better.

After eating what I could of supper, I went to my room and lay on the bed. But instead of crying, I slept. Very late Dad, or maybe it was Aunt Mary, came in, took off my shoes, and put a blanket over me. I woke when it was just faintly light in the east beyond the tall stacks of the mill. Then I hid under the covers and cried and cried until long after the sun was up. How could it happen? How could it happen to me?

Late Friday afternoon Aunt Mary drove my cousins and me to the funeral home. My cousins watched me stealthily. They were all younger and I couldn't talk to any of them—not really.

Dad and Uncle Jerry were already at the funeral home greeting the people who came to the visitation. Awful, sad organ music played softly over hidden speakers. Two dark, shiny caskets sat at the far end of the room surrounded by tall vases of flowers. The lids were sealed. The car had burned and no amount of the mortician's time or skill could restore the look of humanity to those bodies. I tried not to think about what Mom and Roxy looked like inside those boxes. But Dad knew.

Near the caskets Grandma sat with Mom's two older sisters standing beside her. Grandma was old and sick even then and she died a few months later. I went to her awkwardly, waiting my turn as my aunts talked to people quietly, introduced Grandma, who hardly looked up, then shooed them gently away. When I stood before her, she looked up, her red, watery eyes nearly hidden in the deep wrinkles on her face. She didn't say anything, just took me into that fragile lilac-scented, old lady's hug. I stood there, then clumsily put my arms around her.

After a minute Aunt June gently separated us. "Mother, I'd like you to meet . . ." Aunt Meg led me away, explaining carefully that Grandma was very tired and we must be careful not to upset her. I stood with Dad and Uncle Jerry for a while. I couldn't believe how strong, at times almost a little hearty, the two men seemed as they greeted the people who came with sympathy. Everyone seemed to say the same kind of things. Things like: "We're so sorry." "She was a wonderful woman." "Anything we can do, John." "Please come for dinner soon . . ."

The few kids who came were awkward. Some of them hid behind their parents, attempting only a faint "Hi, Steve." The braver kids talked only about school. Their parents said things to me like: "You'll be a big help to your father." "You're very brave." "Your mother would be proud of you. . . ." But when Mr. Ohm came by, he only shook my hand. I didn't really know him then, but I liked him a lot after that night. He hadn't tried to say the unsayable.

Aunt Mary got all the kids from the family together about eight o'clock and took us home. In the hour and a half I'd been at the funeral home, I hadn't gone within ten feet of the caskets.

That night the family gathered at the house. Grandma rested in the spare bedroom upstairs while my aunts and uncles talked. There were three families, four if you counted Dad and me. My older cousins were nice, but pretty much stayed with the adults. My younger cousins, allowed this night to stay up late, treated it almost like a party and had to be constantly hushed by their parents. I felt alone in the middle of it all. After a while I slipped into the library and curled up in a chair. Dad's big desk sat against one wall and I thought of crawling into the deep cave beneath it where the varnish had been worn from the floor by the soles of Dad's shoes during the long hours he'd sat at the desk correcting all the years of lab reports and test papers.

After a long while I heard the people who were staying overnight at motels start getting ready to leave. Nearby Dad called my name. I didn't move or reply. He stepped inside the door and flipped on the light. "Steven, you've got to come and say good night."

"Why, Dad? No one will miss me."

"Yes, they will. Come on, now. It'll just take a few minutes."

"I don't feel like it, Dad."

He stood quiet for a moment. "Steven, there are some things we have to do. Some things that are expected. Your grandmother will be down in a minute and she will especially want to see you. It's tough, I know, but it's one of those things we have to do." We looked at each other for a long moment. Dad's eyes were red-rimmed and bloodshot. Then I got up and went with him.

The church was full, but I didn't look back at the crowd as I followed Dad to the front pew. Behind me Mom's sisters brought Grandma. Aunt Mary and my youngest cousins were already lined up in the pew behind ours.

The minister led the procession down the aisle from the rear door of the church. Roxy's casket, only slightly smaller than Mom's, came first, wheeled by three of my cousins and three of her friends from school. My three uncles, Mr. Ohm, and my two oldest cousins served as pallbearers for Mom.

I don't remember much of the prayers or the hymns. I remember Grandma shaking so hard her daughters had to support her, and Dad standing beside me, his hands gripping the rail in front so hard his knuckles turned white. And I remember staring at those two shiny boxes covered with dark-purple palls and the feeling beneath my numbness that any second I would start screaming and have to run from the church. But I was hemmed in on either side and all around, and a person did what was expected—even if the charred bodies in those boxes were his mother and sister.

158

At last we stood in the cemetery in the cool afternoon, big tumbling clouds hiding the sun, then letting it break through to wash warm light over us. The breeze ruffled the clothes of the people gathering around. Drapes covered the stands over the graves, but now and again the breeze would lift a corner so I could look into the darkness below.

The pallbearers carried the caskets up the low grassy rise from the drive where the hearses sat, long, shiny, and black. The funeral director gave the pallbearers quick, soft directions as they placed the caskets on the stands. Then he laid a spray of flowers on each casket. The breeze rustled the white flowers.

The minister said two more prayers, then shook sand from his bell-shaped, silver shaker over the caskets intoning, "We commend to Almighty God our sisters and we commit their bodies to the ground, earth to earth, ashes to ashes, dust to dust." I felt my legs start quivering as if the breeze that caught and blew that sand had slipped inside me. But one does what is expected, and when we turned away, I forced my legs to carry me back down the hill. Grandma stood beside the limousine, leaning heavily on Aunt Meg's arm, too old to climb that gentle hill for the final farewell to her daughter and granddaughter.

Our lives went on. That was what was expected, right? The relatives left and Dad went back to senior high and I returned to junior high. That summer Dad sold the house and most of our furniture and belongings, and we moved into the apartment. Pretty soon about the only thing to remind us of Mom and Roxy was the picture on the corner table and the emptiness. Somewhere in that time we started to fight a lot. My grades hadn't been too hot before and they started down that next fall and kept going down after that.

The Wart thing started in eighth grade and I began to feel more lonely than ever. And as Mr. Ohm reminded me much later, Dad too seemed lonelier, cutting himself off from old friends, hiding in his work, hiding behind that grim, businesslike mask he wore more and more. And each anniversary we went to the cemetery to lay a wreath on the graves and to immerse ourselves in our grief once again.

My feet and my thoughts had taken me far from downtown and the library. I was now within a few blocks of Trish's house. I walked the rest of the way debating. I'd laid so much on her in recent weeks, was it fair to ask her to listen to any more? Besides, she'd probably be gone somewhere on a Saturday. Still, I kept walking. I can always turn back, I thought, but of course I didn't.

She was sitting on the front porch steps in a sweatshirt and shorts. God, she looked good. Maybe not beautiful like Cummings' girlfriend, but I'd take Trish anytime. The family car wasn't in the driveway. Good. Trish's folks were nice people, but I didn't want to talk to them today. I waved and she waved back. "Hi, what are you doing up here?"

"Just walking, this seemed as good a direction as any."

"Wow, what a compliment." She giggled.

I blushed a little. "I didn't mean it that way." I sat down beside her. "Do you mind?"

"Of course not." She nudged me. "I haven't seen you since you became a hero."

"What? Oh, ya. No big deal. We were just there."

"Have you heard anything?"

"Dad called the Phantom this morning. Mattson's still in intensive care, but I guess he's going to pull through."

"That's good. I was proud of you when I heard."

"Thanks, but it wasn't a big deal."

"Have it your way. You heroes are always modest, I hear."

"Hey, you're pretty frisky this morning."

"And why not? Look at this beautiful day. Makes a girl just ready for romance."

"Oh, ya? Well, let me know if I can help out."

She laughed and for a second her eyes seemed to change just a little. "Maybe I'll do that sometime." Before I could think of a reply, she jumped up. "Want a Coke?"

"Sure."

160

She went inside. I stared down at my algebra book and folder on the bottom step. So much to do. If I could pass, get into Capstone, and get that camp job, maybe I would have a chance at a little romance with her. But first there was this afternoon. I ought to leave. You can't win a girl by always telling her your troubles, Wart. Be cheerful for a few minutes, drink your Coke, and go. Let her enjoy her Saturday.

She came back out, handed me a can, and sat. "So what are you going to do today? Not just algebra, I hope."

"Well, no. Dad and I are going up to put a wreath on the graves of my mother and sister."

"Oh, that's right. You told me that today was the, ah, anniversary. I forgot. I'm sorry."

"Don't be. It's not a big deal."

"Stop saying that all the time. It's a refrain with you. It *is* a big deal, isn't it?"

I nodded. "Ya, I guess so." There was a pause. "I shouldn't always be telling you my problems."

"I don't mind."

"It's just that, well, you said it last Saturday—it's been a long time. Sometimes I try to remember them, picture them doing things, and it's hard. And when I do remember an incident, I'm just a little boy in the scene. And I'm not a little boy anymore. Anyway, it's all pretty confusing."

"What do you remember best?"

"That's funny too, because they're mostly little things like, I don't know, like going to the fair and riding on the Tilt-a-Whirl with my sister. One of her girlfriends was along, but was afraid to get on, so she watched with Dad and Mom while Roxy and I rode. Then she decided she did want to ride, so Dad paid for two more tickets, and Mom, Roxy, and Dad stood watching and laughing while I rode with Melody."

"That sounds like a good memory."

"It isn't, really. I got sick."

She laughed. "Oh, that's awful. With everybody watching?" I nodded. She put a hand on my arm. "Oh, Steve, you can't be embarrassed about that still?"

"Well, I am a little, and I can't understand why so many things I remember are like that—times when I was embarrassed or angry with them or just not very happy."

"There must have been a lot of happy times too."

"Ya, there were. Lots of them. But it seems I remember the bad times best. This may sound terrible, and maybe I'm a terrible person for saying it, but a lot of the time I didn't like Mom or Roxy very much. Like Mom was always poking me, and I hated that. If she wanted me to sit up straight at the table, she'd poke me. If she wanted me to hurry up, she'd poke me. Usually, she wouldn't say anything, she'd just poke me. The first Sunday after I was confirmed, I stood in line for communion ahead of her, thinking all the things you're supposed to think, and she started poking me. I didn't know what she wanted, so I didn't do anything, and then she kind of pushed me in the direction of the other line. I didn't know you were supposed to go to the other line if it was a lot shorter. So right there in front of the whole church, she was poking and pushing me. Not hard, but damn it, why didn't she just whisper to me? I wasn't exactly in the right frame of mind when I got to the rail. I was mad as hell."

Trish laughed again, but more gently this time. "I don't blame you. I'd have been angry too."

"But doesn't that make me an awful person, always remembering the bad things? I mean, Mom was wonderful, but some of the times I remember best are the times I didn't like her."

"I don't think that makes you an awful person. You're just remembering things that made a big impression on you. I think you're blaming yourself for not always liking her just because she's gone."

I nodded. "That's part of it, I guess. But I should have been nicer to both of them, not always a little brat."

"You weren't always a little brat, were you?"

"Maybe not, but a lot of the time I was."

"So, you're human. You can't blame yourself for that."

I grimaced. "You ought to be a shrink."

She laughed again and squeezed my arm. "Tell me more."

I did. I told her about when I'd talked Mom into letting me stay up until eight-thirty instead of going to bed at eight like Roxy. After all, I was three years older and deserved the privilege. Mom had finally given in and said all right, if I was in bed at eight, I could read or play quietly for a half-hour. I'd felt big and grown up until two nights later when I'd gotten up to go to the bathroom and, passing Roxy's room, seen her sitting in bed coloring. She'd been given the same privilege. I'd felt horribly, unspeakably betrayed and staying up that extra half-hour was no longer any fun.

And I told Trish about how Roxy always seemed to get the blame put on me, even when we'd both been at fault. Yet, whenever I'd complain to Mom about it, she'd always say that Roxy was "just a little girl." And Roxy's pout at those times! Mom couldn't see it, but I could. Roxy's eyes would be laughing. Later, when Mom was out of the room, Roxy would sometimes laugh at me outright. Once I'd chased her, determined to pay her back. I'd kicked at her and missed, and my foot went through a pane of glass in the door to the backyard. I didn't get dessert for a week and had to work off every cent it cost to replace that stupid window.

Trish understood and consoled me with laughter. And now that I'd started to actually tell about those things, they *were* kind of funny and I began to laugh too. I told her more stories—and not only about the bad times, but also the good and fun times we'd had as a family. Like the camping trip when we'd forgotten the tent poles and Mom had said, "What the heck, we'll just put on lots of mosquito dope and sleep under the stars." And we had, talking and joking beside the fire until midnight. Or the time we were washing the car and Mom got silly and shoved the hose down the back of Dad's pants. It had been an epic water fight that eventually involved all four of us and a couple of the neighbor kids too. So many times and so long ago.

I sobered when the noon whistle blew at the mill. Time to be getting home. "Well, thanks, I've got to go."

"I'm glad you came. It made my morning."

"I'm glad I came too. Things are always a little brighter after talking to you."

"I'm glad. I'll see you in church tomorrow."

"Okay." I started down the driveway.

"Steve . . ." I turned. "Good luck this afternoon. And—this is your shrink speaking—the past is, you know, over."

"I know."

We stopped to pick up the wreath at the greenhouse that sits in a quiet neighborhood on the bluff overlooking the center of Brandt Mills. Dad went in and I leaned against the car looking down on the city. In the distance through the haze from the great stacks of the mill, I could make out the shining river twisting south in the calm, sunny day.

Roxy. How little I really thought about her. She'd be thirteen and probably more of a pain in the ass than ever. I smiled at the thought. Ya, she'd be driving us all nuts. But she'd never be thirteen and Mom would never be forty-two. Time had left them behind. I closed my eyes and felt the warm sun on my face and the light breeze that blew through the new leaves on the trees. The season had turned; summer was here.

Dad came out and we drove the last few blocks to the cemetery. We climbed the grassy rise to their graves in silence. I helped Dad remove the cellophane from the wreath and set it on a stand between the simple brass markers. A wreath of pink, white, and yellow flowers—it was pretty. He stepped back and we bowed our heads. We stood like that for a long minute.

"Dad."

"Yes, Steven."

"Dad, I still miss them a lot, but it's been three years now." I took a deep breath. God, this was tough. "Dad, maybe it's time we let them go." I looked at him, afraid to see his face turn angry. Instead, two big tears rolled down his cheeks. He took out his handkerchief and dabbed at his eyes. "I'm sorry, Dad, I didn't mean—"

He shook his head. "No. You're right. I know it's time. I've known it for a long time. It's just that the parting is so damn hard . . . like the funeral all over again."

"Dad, we can't hold on to them forever." My voice was thick and tears came to my eyes. "It's time we really said . . . good-bye."

Neither one of us could talk any more. For a few minutes we stood on that little hill in the bright May sunshine, then Dad reached down to adjust the wreath once more and together we walked back to the waiting car and the rest of our lives.

14

As finals came closer, the days seemed to speed by. I couldn't find enough hours to do all I needed to do. I'd never studied so hard. I immersed myself completely in the work, forgetting nearly everything but preparing for finals.

Mattson was in intensive care for nearly a week, and another week passed before Dad and I went to see him one Wednesday after school. He lay in a big white bed paging through a magazine. His cheeks above the beard were still pale, but remembering how he'd looked when they'd wheeled him out, I was surprised to see him looking so good.

"John, Steve, it's good to see you." He reached up and we took his hand in turn—a hand that seemed cold, chilled somehow by the frigid hospital atmosphere.

"You're looking good, Dan," Dad said. "I'm sorry we didn't come sooner, but we weren't sure you were ready for visitors yet."

"Just the last couple of days. Sit down. Sit down. Not much for accommodations here." Only a single chair stood by the bed, so I let Dad take it and perched on the ventilator under the window.

"So how do you feel?" Dad asked.

"Oh, a little rocky yet. For a couple of days they weren't sure I was going to make it at all, but I'm feeling better now.

Bypass surgery this August probably. I guess I won't be playing any golf this summer." He smiled faintly.

"Well, you're looking good." They both seemed at a loss for words.

"How are things at the plant?" Mattson asked.

"Oh, pretty much as usual. With finals coming up, lots of work to do. It's springtime and the kids are getting a little hard to handle."

"Happens every year." Mattson chuckled, but it sounded weak.

They talked for a few more minutes about school and then Dad rose. "Well, Dan, we've got to be going. Just came to see how you were." He reached out and took Mattson's hand again.

"Thanks for coming." He took my hand next. "I understand you and Cummings saved my life."

I shrugged, embarrassed. "We were just there. We did what we could."

He shook my hand a little harder. "I'm glad you did. Thanks."

As usual, I was the last one out of the library, leaving only when the aide put the cover on her typewriter and went for her coat, giving me a dirty look on the way. If I wasn't camping there every afternoon, she'd probably try to slip out ten minutes early, but I figured she was paid until four o'clock and didn't need any breaks from me.

In the lab, I settled down at my usual table near the fish tanks and the salamander jungle to study until Dad was ready to go. I was still driving us home, so there wasn't any opportunity to catch a ride with one of the guys. I really didn't care either; I was happy to be by myself these days. Finals were too important to allow any distractions.

Dad came out of his office, tossed a letter on my table, and set about straightening the room. I glanced at the postmark: Milwaukee. Who on earth? I tore it open and unfolded a piece of lined notebook paper with a tight scrawl on one side. It was from Keith. I'll be damned, I thought.

May 15

Dear Steve,

Had to write this care of your old man since I didn't have your address.

I ran into a couple of the guys over the weekend and heard all the news. They said you and Cummings saved Mattson's butt. We laughed about that since it ain't often jocks and dirts get together on anything—especially saving an assistant principal's life. God, that guy is a hard ass. Still, I'm glad he's going to be okay.

I'm also glad you're still hanging in. I've thought about you quite a few times since I've been down here and wondered how you were doing. Don't let the bastards get you down like they did poor Perry. Stick it out and then tell them to go to hell.

Me? I'm okay. I had to get out of ol' Brandt Mills. The downers were really beginning to screw up my head, and things at home just couldn't get much worse. That's a story I'll tell you sometime. Anyway, I sold my car for a few bucks, then hitched down here. I got a job busing dishes and crashed with a couple of guys I knew from last summer. Busing dishes is a bummer, but next week I start an apprenticeship program in carpentry. It won't pay much, but it'll keep me going through the summer. Maybe I'll even stick with it. Have to try it first.

Well, I'm not much of a letter writer, but I did want to tell you I'm still alive and to wish you luck with finals and all. Drop me a note when you have time or, better yet, stop and see me if you come through.

Take care,
Keith

His address followed. I folded the sheet and stuck it in my pocket. So Keith was making it. That was great—somehow I'd doubted that he would.

"Who's the letter from?" Dad was pulling on his coat awkwardly.

"A friend, Keith Miller."

Dad glanced at me sharply. "Oh? And how's young Mr. Miller doing?"

"He's doing real good, Dad. I think he's getting his act straightened out."

Dad stood for a moment, then said quietly, "That's good. I'm glad. Well, ready to go?"

"Sure." I gathered up my stuff.

Cummings caught me in the hall in the middle of the morning. "Here." He shoved an envelope at me.

"What's this?" I opened it. Inside were five twenty-dollar bills.

"It's all there. Just put it away."

"Jim, you didn't . . . This isn't yours, is it?"

"Are you kidding?" He grinned at me. "It came from the right place. They won't be doing that kind of thing again."

"I hope you didn't hurt anybody."

"Nothing permanent. Mostly pride."

"Well, thanks. You doing okay?"

"Me? Sure. Just rolling along. Take care." He sauntered off.

What was I going to do with the money? Giving it to Dad would only prompt a lot of questions. Finally, I stuck it in another envelope and mailed it to our apartment with a typewritten note. "We're very sorry about what our son did. He won't do it again." Dad was delighted and I was off the hook.

The night after he got the envelope, I decided to talk to him while we were doing dishes. "Dad, since Mr. Mattson's heart attack I've gotten to know Jim Cummings a little. He's not really a bad guy, not like Vanik and some of the others."

He nodded. "I've always thought Cummings was the pick

of that bunch. He swaggers a bit, but he'll grow out of it. Fine quarterback, that's for sure."

"He's actually kind of modest about that."

"That's pretty hard to believe."

"Well, he is. And, Dad, he told me that no one in his crowd was behind wrecking the Buick. I believe him, too."

He raised his eyebrows. "Oh? Well, that's good to hear."

"He also thinks all the jock/dirt thing has gone too far and the Toad and Wart crap too."

Dad glanced up sharply from drying some forks, but I was committed now and kept going.

"He wants to cool things off, but he says it would help if maybe you, ah, just took it a little easier."

"Steven . . ."

"Believe me, Dad, I'm not criticizing. But if you could just talk to kids a little more quietly when you catch them breaking some little rule, maybe they wouldn't get so mad or be so quick to call you Toad later on."

He laughed harshly. "I don't think things are quite that simple. They've been calling me Toad for a long time. I expect to hear it the day I retire."

"I'm not saying the names would go away completely, Dad. Someone will call me Wart the day I graduate, but maybe it wouldn't be quite so often if we just cooled it a little." I rinsed out the sink. "Dad, I'm not putting you down, but think about it, okay?" He nodded. "I've got to study now. I'll see you later." I was surprised he'd taken it so well. Maybe it had done some good.

I dug through my locker. I had to make sure I had everything I needed for studying over the last weekend before finals.

Jeff came up. "Hi, Steve, I haven't seen much of you lately."

"I've been kinda busy getting ready for finals. How you doin'?"

170

"Okay, I guess. Say, you know I stopped coming to speech."

"Ya, I noticed."

"It was just more than I could handle. Do you think if I asked, I might get an incomplete instead of flunking?"

"I don't know. Why don't you talk to your counselor? Maybe if you explained how bummed out you were about Perry's accident, they might let you make it up next year."

Jeff nodded. "Ya, maybe I'll do that. Still, I might not be back next year, anyway. They're moving some of the company executives around and my old man thinks he may get transferred to another mill."

"Oh, ya? How do you feel about that?"

"I hope it happens; I'd like a new start somewhere else. You know, I've kind of been avoiding you and a lot of the guys recently." I nodded. "After you took that swing at Cummings, I started to think, Wow, I'll be the next one to hype out. So, I just quit all the craziness. I'm sorry if it seemed like I was pissed at you or something."

"I didn't think that. I figured you just wanted to be alone for a while. Don't worry about it."

"Ya, well, we'll see you around." He started away, then turned. "Steve, we've just got to get away from this goddamn jock/dirt thing! If some other guys want to fight, let 'em. But not me. To hell with it! It isn't worth it. It never was. I quit."

We stood looking at each other in the deserted hall. "I know," I said quietly "I already quit."

Finals began on Monday. For three days we had open campus, with everyone following the exam schedule rather than the usual class schedule. My speech final came first. They'd hired a substitute to take Mattson's place, but the assignment was still the same: a seven- to ten-minute persuasive speech arguing one side of a controversial topic. We were supposed to follow the recommendations in the handbook on argumentation and debate, an incredibly boring piece of garbage I'd finally fought my way through. Even tougher was preparing the required audiovisual aids. We had lots of choices: slides, videotapes, recordings, transparencies, and so forth. But if something went wrong with the AV stuff, we had to finish any way we could. It was bound to prove exciting.

Since I knew more about cars than anything else, I looked around for a topic concerning them, finally deciding to argue that American car companies were at fault for most of their problems and shouldn't be protected with quotas on foreign imports. I spent four hours in the AV lab putting my graphs and stuff on transparencies and was pretty happy with the result. Maybe the better students would have flashier audiovisuals, but mine should do more than well enough.

I'd traded speaking numbers with Lorie, so I could get the speech out of the way quick. Better to go up early than sit around and sweat out the wait. Still, I was plenty nervous when I got to the front. What irony if I couldn't get a C in speech after saving the regular teacher's life. I had no idea how the sub would grade. His manner didn't exactly put anyone at ease. He was about six-four and ran the class like a military drill. Was there something about teaching speech that made a man mean?

Things started off smoothly, even if I did have a brief moment of panic when I couldn't find my third transparency for a few seconds. In all I had seven, and when I got the sixth on the overhead projector, I took a quick look at my watch. Six and a half minutes gone—right on schedule. Now to really give it to the car companies. The light on the screen died. I looked quickly at the wall socket. No, the cord was still plugged in and the fan in the projector whirred peacefully. The damn bulb had burned out! I gave the projector a tentative tap—nothing. I glanced at the sub. He was watching me, eyebrows a little raised. Except for the whir of the fan and the sound of a couple of kids shifting nervously, the room was dead quiet.

I grinned. "I wonder if this machine was made in Detroit." Everybody, including the sub, laughed. I turned to the board and, as carefully as I could with a shaking hand, drew my last two graphs. I tried to continue speaking while I drew. I flubbed one point and had to correct myself, but I finally finished and went to my seat. I was dripping with sweat.

Hal leaned over and whispered, "Nice going. You pulled it off, but what am I supposed to do with my transparencies?"

The sub had gone to the front and had the projector open. About half the kids were whispering nervously. Most had planned to use transparencies, too. "Well, it looks like we need a new bulb. Young fella"—he looked at me—"will you run to AV and get one?" I hopped up. "By the way, you did well. Now, class, when something like that happens, try to laugh it off and finish as well as you can. Let's fill out our grade recommendations and we'll conspire in private while he gets the bulb." He winked at me as I headed for the door. It was certain now—speech was safe. One down, five to go.

The English exam that afternoon was tough, much too long, but I hacked my way through it and finished just as the bell rang. Many of the kids pushed their papers away and started griping about not having enough time. That cinched it. Old lady Rawls probably wouldn't flunk anyone, at least no one who'd gotten done.

Auto mechanics on Tuesday morning was a snap. Mr. Ohm joked about the exam. It was really just a formality to him. What counted was how you could handle a wrench. When I handed in my paper at the end of the period, he grinned at me. "How'd it go?"

"Okay. I wasn't too sure about a couple of the questions on transmissions."

"Don't worry about it. How are your other tests going?"

"Okay, so far. The tough ones are coming up."

"Well, stay calm. Your dad says you've been working your butt off. I'm sure you'll do okay."

I'd needed that and felt good as I studied through the middle of the day in the library. The phys-ed final was a two-part exam you could take anytime. The written part on the first-aid manual worried me, but by two o'clock I figured I was ready and walked down to the lecture room.

A couple dozen kids sat spread about the room. The supervisor, a not very bright student teacher, handed me a test and pointed to a seat in the row in front of Vanik and a couple of other jocks. Cummings and two more guys sat in the row behind them.

I'd finished about half the exam and was feeling pretty good about it when Vanik leaned over. "Hey, Wart, shove your answer sheet where I can see it." I ignored him and kept my test hidden in front of my body. "Hey, Wart, move your sheet or I'll beat your goddamn head in after class."

"Do your own test, Tom, and leave Steve alone." Cummings' soft, Western drawl was barely audible where I sat two rows ahead of him.

"But, Jim . . ." Vanik protested.

"You heard me. It ain't his fault you didn't read the book."

I finished the test, trying to calm my pounding heart, handed it in, and retreated to the library. I hadn't done super, but well enough. The physical half of the phys-ed test was a timed two-mile run, but I figured I'd let that go until last, rather than running alongside the jocks, who'd troop down to the gym as soon as they'd finished the first-aid test.

Fate and the computer had put my two toughest exams on the last day: history in the morning and algebra in the afternoon. I reviewed as much of the history as I could late Tuesday afternoon. I had to reserve the evening for algebra. After supper I called Trish. This would be my last opportunity to talk to her for I wasn't sure how long. Her last exam was in the morning and she was leaving in the afternoon for a week's vacation with her family before she started work at camp.

"Hi, Steve. How are things going?"

"Okay, I guess. Dad and I are going to work on algebra tonight."

"I know you'll do okay."

"I wish I had your confidence." There was an awkward pause. "So, are you looking forward to camp?"

"Sure am. I got a letter today and I'm now a senior counselor. And they gave me a raise too."

"Congratulations. Well, have fun. I may see you there."

"I really hope so, Steve. Work hard tonight, huh?"

"Ya, I will. Good night, now."

"Good night."

It hadn't been much of a conversation. I was just too tense. Worry about Trish later. I had to get at the algebra.

It was past eleven o'clock. I dropped my pencil and put my head in my hands. I couldn't remember how to do it.

Dad sighed. "You were headed in the right direction. Now watch, Steven." He finished the problem. "Try another."

I picked up my pencil and tried again. My head ached and my eyes burned, but I had to keep at it. I got to the end of the problem and glanced up at Dad.

He compressed his lips and shook his head. "Not quite." I tried again, forcing myself to think carefully. "Okay. There you got it." I leaned back, closing my eyes. We'd been at it for going on six hours. Dad paged ahead in the book. After a minute, he said, "Well, I think that's enough for tonight, Steven."

I opened my eyes. "There aren't any more nights, Dad."

"I know, but you're too tired to absorb much now. It's better that you get a good night's sleep. In the morning we'll review a little more and then I think you'll be able to pass." I started to object, but my fatigue overwhelmed me and I nodded. At the door he paused. "It's been a long haul, hasn't it?"

"Ya, a long one."

"Well, you've come a long way. Farther than I think you know. I'm proud of you, son. Just go to bed now. You'll do fine." But he didn't sound very confident, and neither was I.

First thing Wednesday morning I took the history exam and found it surprisingly easy. Somewhere along the line I'd picked up most of the important points and now I whipped through it in time to get in fifteen minutes studying algebra at the end of the period. Everything depended on the algebra final now—only phys ed after that, and I could run two miles well within the time. I didn't see how I could get less than a C− in any of my other courses now, but I'd need a C on the algebra final to get a D for the year. With my B in auto mechanics my grade point would average out to a low C, good enough to get into Capstone.

To my surprise, Trish was waiting near the door to Miss Thomas' room. She smiled. "I thought you might need a last-minute vote of confidence. How do you feel?"

"Scared. Real scared. I wish you could take it for me."

"I think they'd notice." She giggled, but I could only manage a sickly smile. My stomach felt terrible. "Well, try not to be nervous." She jumped up on tiptoes and gave me a quick kiss on the cheek. "For luck." She hurried away.

My God, she'd kissed me in the hall with all sorts of people around! I looked after her in amazement. After a few stunned seconds, I went into the room. Okay, Wart, let's get our shit together.

Miss Thomas distributed the test, announced a couple of typographical corrections, and we began. Tough. God, it was tough! I fought through one problem after another, painstakingly checking my work. I had to pick up every possible point. Halfway through the period I was only a little better than a third done with the test. I worked faster, checking my solutions less and less often as the minutes slid by. When she said, "Time," I was still a page short of the end. I leaned back and groaned. Had it been enough? I wasn't sure. It would be tight. Too damned tight.

My tennis shoes slapped on the hard, varnished boards of the gym floor. Damn it! Now I remembered how to solve those three problems I'd left blank early in the test. Stupid. Last night I could have solved them without even thinking. So unbearably stupid!

I jogged down the straightaway past Mr. Lindon and one of the student teachers. They sat at a table with a half-dozen stopwatches and charts in front of them, checking off each runner as he passed. It seemed a cumbersome system. "Half done, Michaels, looking good," Lindon called.

Oh, screw you, I thought. I can count and I've been watching the clock since I started running. I had no intention of doing more than the minimum, but as my feet brought me into the second mile, I started to run a little faster. Damn that algebra! How stupid I'd been. I'd known it better than that.

At a mile and a half I was running hard, putting my whole body into it. Screw 'em, I thought, I've done my best. If a few dumb problems in algebra keep me out of Capstone, then let them keep their damn diploma. I'll just drop out.

A mile and three-quarters was coming up and I let it out. Screw 'em! I don't need a C average to tell me that I can work just as hard, face just as much, and be just as good as anyone else. Blood spouted from my nose. Oh, shit! I grabbed the front of my shirt and crushed it to my nose.

"Hey, Michaels, drop out. You've done enough." Lindon waved me toward the sidelines, but I shook my head and ran on. I still had four laps to do.

The next time around he stuck out a hand to stop me, but I dodged him and kept going. After that he just stood and watched as I gutted it out. I couldn't run very fast now. Other runners passed me, then glanced back curiously. But I crossed the finish line two minutes short of the maximum time and dropped to a walk.

Lindon stood slowly shaking his head. "You didn't have to do that."

"Yes, I did." I pulled off my shirt. It was soaked a bright red and I felt the other kids watching me as I walked to the locker room. I didn't give a damn anymore. School was out. I'd finished as hard as I could.

For the first time in weeks I walked home. Dad's cast had been removed Monday and now his wrist was bound in an

Ace bandage, but he could drive and I no longer had to wait for him.

When I came into the apartment, I thought automatically of what I had to study. But I was done now, and suddenly I felt an extraordinary emptiness. The night, the week ahead, my very life itself seemed to fall away in front of me, an endless, echoing void. I walked through the apartment nervously, then flopped down and gazed at the blank screen of the TV.

I must have sat there for twenty minutes, my mind whirling, trying to focus on something. Then I got up, turned on the TV, and went to the kitchen for a Coke. I'd failed. I knew it. I just hadn't done enough of that algebra exam. Miss Thomas would add up her precious points and flunk me for sure. I'd blown it! All the weeks of effort had been wasted. Good for nothing!

Dad usually stays even later than normal during exam week, so I almost jumped out of my socks when he came in. I'd been a million miles away, lost in a black gulf of depression. "How'd it go?" he asked quietly.

"Not so good. I don't think I made it, Dad."

"Didn't you understand it?"

"I understood most of it, Dad. I just couldn't do it fast enough. I probably left a quarter of it blank, counting the problems I skipped."

"Hmmm . . . well, I'm going to call Sylvia."

"No, Dad. I don't want to beg."

"I'm not going to beg. I just want to see if she's got the test graded yet."

He walked into the kitchen and I heard him dial the phone. "Hello, Sylvia. John Michaels here. Have you graded the algebra final yet? . . . Yes, I understand it's early yet. We're just a little concerned. . . . Yes, of course. . . . We're not asking any favors, just concerned. . . . Yes, thank you. I'd appreciate it."

He came back in. "She doesn't have them done yet, but she said she'd call as soon as she knows your grade." I nodded. "Well, do you want to go out to eat?"

"I'm not very hungry, Dad."

"Well, I'm going to fix a snack. Maybe you'll feel like going out later."

The phone rang about eight o'clock. I was still sitting in front of the TV, too listless to move. Dad answered. "Yes, Sylvia. . . . Yes. . . . Thanks. . . . Yes, he certainly did. Thanks so much for calling." The phone plopped into the carriage and Dad whooped. I leapt up in alarm. The next second he was there pumping my hand and trying to slap me on the back with his bad arm. "You did it, Steven! A solid C. She says you'll get a C− for the year on the basis of improvement."

I was thunderstruck. So I had made it! I couldn't think if I wanted to laugh or yell or cry. So I just stood there trying to comprehend it.

The gym was hot and stuffy. We sat, all 1,100 of us, sweating through the final agony, the end-of-the-year assembly. That morning the seniors had practiced for the graduation ceremony while the rest of us cleaned out lockers, turned in books, got next year's schedules finally approved (Capstone!), paid library fines, and were generally bored to hell. Now at eleven o'clock we'd joined the seniors to hear about the scholarship winners and all the other superstars of the school.

The valedictorian spoke, a smug kid who'd always been so far above everyone else that most of his own class hardly knew him. Carry on the traditions of Brandt Mills High, etc. Tradition my ass, I thought. Get on with it.

Finally, it was time for the Phantom. He thanked everybody and everybody's third cousin for making this another successful year at Brandt Mills High, gave us a quick pep talk, and then paused for a second, shuffling his papers on the podium. "We have a brief and very special presentation before we start honoring our scholarship winners. Then we'll let you all get some fresh air." There was a smattering of applause, and he grinned. Spare us the jokes, for God's sake, I thought. "Mrs. Audrey Gray of the Brandt Mills Chapter of the American Red Cross has an award for two of our young men who saved the life of our fine acting assistant principal, Mr. Daniel Mattson, when he suffered a heart attack in his office a few weeks ago. Will James Cummings and Steven Michaels please come forward."

Why hadn't anyone told us? I wasn't ready for this. I succeeded in maneuvering down the tight row over all the feet and down from the bleachers. Cummings was getting out of the junior section nearer the platform. I hurried to the front and climbed the stairs, intensely aware of all the eyes on me.

Mrs. Gray, a tiny, pleasant-faced woman, waited for me to get to Cummings' side before she started. "The Brandt Mills Chapter of the American Red Cross takes great pleasure in awarding these two courageous young men with lifesaving certificates for their prompt and effective administration of cardiopulmonary resuscitation on the afternoon of May sixth, when Assistant Principal . . ." She talked on, describing what we'd done, more or less, praising the school for its CPR program, asking all students to tell their parents about the Red Cross evening classes, and finally returning to praise us again.

Once I flicked a quick glance at Cummings, who winked back, but kept a straight face. She finished, handed us framed certificates, and shook our hands while the kids applauded. The Phantom stood and shook our hands too. Only when we started to descend the steps did I notice that everyone was standing and the applause was louder than ever. I blushed crimson. Maybe they were clapping for Cummings more than me—the school hero notching another honor—but I didn't care.

Near the doors a big kid was standing by himself clapping furiously. My God, it was Fred! He looked thin and his dark skin seemed almost pale. Our eyes met. I gave him a friendly smile and a wave, not knowing exactly why. He bobbed his head up and down, trying to grin. Cummings gave me a slap on the shoulder and went over to talk to him. I climbed back into the bleachers as the applause settled and the Phantom started announcing the scholarship winners.

180

* * *

That evening I took the car and drove around town. Lots of kids were out partying, but I didn't feel much like it. I just drove slowly around, looking again at the town where I'd spent sixteen years of my life. For the first time I'd be out on my own. Two and a half months away from Brandt Mills—and Dad, although somehow that part didn't seem very important anymore.

I wished Trish was with me. Hell, I hadn't even been able to tell her I'd passed algebra. But I'd tell her that in a few days—and maybe more. If that boyfriend of hers had just dropped down an elevator shaft or something. . . .

After a while I stopped at the roller rink where there was a dance, but after an hour I had a headache from the heat, smoke, and noise. I drove home slowly past the brightly lighted mill, then into our dark, quiet neighborhood.

Dad was sitting in his usual chair in front of the TV, a can of beer at his elbow. "Hi, I didn't expect you home so early. I thought you'd carouse half the night."

"Didn't feel much like it." I sat down on the couch.

"Not much of a movie, some pilot for a series that didn't make it."

"Ya, I've seen it. It's stupid."

Dad turned it off and we sat in silence for a few minutes. "So, what now?"

"I'm not sure, Dad. Mind if I have a beer?"

"Go ahead. Bring me one too."

I went to the refrigerator and got out the last two beers. On the way back I turned on the stereo low and flipped off the overhead light. Only the new lamp on the corner table beside Mom and Roxy's picture lit the room. "Here." I handed him the beer and sat.

"Thanks. Cheers."

We sat listening to the music—soft, distant country music. It matched my mood somehow—songs about things being over, about paying dues. Things had changed. So much of the past was receding now: the grief for Mom and Roxy, the fears about failing, the anger between Dad and me. It had been time for all that to fade, and the future was bright. Yet, sitting beside my father listening to the music, I felt a little sad. Changes.

Finally, I took a deep breath. "I guess I'll pack in the morning, Dad. There's a bus leaving for Minocqua at noon."

"You don't have to, you know. I could drive you up on Sunday."

"I know, but that would be a long drive back with your arm still not right. Besides, I'd like to have a couple of days by myself before I go to work. Get a campsite and do a little fishing. No offense, Dad, but I've got some things to think about."

"I can understand that." He didn't say anything for a couple of minutes. "You're sure about this camp job? You could stay in town and—"

"I'm sure, Dad."

"And the Capstone thing in the fall?"

"Ya, I'm sure about that too."

He nodded. "Well, maybe I can come up this summer for a couple of days. We could go fishing."

"That would be nice, Dad."

We didn't speak for a long time, both lost in our thoughts. Times changing. In ten weeks I'd be back in Brandt Mills starting my junior year. But things would never be the same. Not for me at least. I took the last swallow from the can. "Well, I'm tired. Good night, Dad."

"Good night."

At the door to my room I turned. He was staring into the vacant corner by the TV. Behind him the small lamp on the corner table gave the room a soft light.

15

I hauled back and kicked the front left tire and added a string of cuss words. Magically, the tractor started running smoothly.

"That's it, Steve. Never take any crap from a tractor." Pete Wiesman, Mr. Ohm's friend and the director of Broken Arrow Camp, stood at the shop door, laughing.

"Hi, Pete. This thing is driving me nuts. That's the first time it's run smooth all afternoon."

"Maybe you ought to kick it more or threaten it with a bigger wrench. Let me take a look."

He stuck his pipe in the pocket of his open shirt. His chest was bronzed and the muscles were those of a much younger man. He examined the engine. "What have you done so far?" I told him. "Then I bet it's a jet. They're tricky on these old Fords sometimes."

Twenty minutes later we left the shop laughing. He'd been right, as he almost always is, but he never minds if I don't know everything. In the last month I've learned more about cars, tractors, machines, and tools than I ever learned in class. That's not to criticize Mr. Ohm's auto-mechanics class, but when you work at it every day, you just have to learn faster.

Pete paused, lighting his pipe and looking fondly across the camp to the big pines and the lake beyond. The dinner bell had rung and the campers, kids from tiny to a few nearly my age, were piling out of the cabins to get in line for the evening meal. "So are we going to have the pleasure of your company at supper, or are you off to squire your young lady?"

"I'm going to clean up and head over there. She's off tomorrow on a canoe trip for a week and I want to see her."

"Ah, the other girls better watch out this coming week. Got to run. See you later."

He jogged off, looking more like twenty-six than sixty-six, and I walked on to my cabin. I was happy. I'd miss Trish this next week, but at least she had the evening off and I had both Saturday and Sunday to relax, unless something went wrong with one of the vehicles.

Everyone else had gone to supper already. I share the cabin with two other guys. Mel, the stable hand, is a kid from south of Eau Claire who had to move into town when the family farm got sold. He loves being out in the country again. We're about the same age and enjoy kidding Pete's nephew, Dick, who's a college sophomore and our cabinmate. Dick's studying accounting and keeps track of the camp finances while helping around the place. We call him Gramps, but he doesn't mind. He's just as even-tempered as his uncle. The three of us get along real well. I got soap, towel, and fresh clothes and walked over to the shower.

In the middle of the lake we let the canoe drift in the wake of the setting sun. A few boats bobbed in the distance along the pine-lined shores as fishermen cast in the shallow waters. Trish turned around and sat watching me. She was dressed in shorts and a halter top. She was good to look at. Her brown hair had bleached almost blond and her skin had turned a deep tan. "You're quiet tonight," she said. "What are you thinking about?"

"Not much. Just enjoying being here and being with one foxy lady."

"Flatterer." She dashed a handful of water in my direction.

"Careful, remember what happened the last time you started that." We laughed. A week before we'd had some practical experience in the art of righting a canoe in deep water. "So, are the ol' Bluebirds ready for the trip?"

"Bluebelles, not Bluebirds, dummy."

"Whatever."

"Oh, they're excited all right. I wish I was."

"You'll enjoy it."

"Oh, sure, but it'll be a lot of work . . . and I'll miss you."

"I could stow away."

"Right, and after three days, all the other counselors would be fighting over you."

"That long, huh?"

"Ooohh, look who's getting a big ego. You better be good while I'm away, fella."

"Scout's honor."

"You're not a Boy Scout."

"I was once. It still counts."

"It better." The sun was almost gone now. "Well, sweets, I guess we'd better go."

I got out my paddle as Trish turned around. "We'll still have time for a walk when we get back, won't we?" I asked.

"Just a few minutes, I'm afraid. The Bluebelles are getting up at five and this girl needs her sleep."

We paddled back in. I admired the muscles on her back and arms moving with each stroke of her paddle. Her boyfriend from last summer was nuts to dump her, I thought. Bless his heart.

We beached the canoe, then carried it up to the long rack where the fading light reflected on the long line of other alumi num hulls. Walking back to where I'd parked the old pickup from Broken Arrow, she asked, "Are you nervous about seeing your dad tomorrow?"

"No, not really. He's pretty relaxed when he's fishing. Besides, we've gotten over a lot of things now. At least I hope so."

We said good-bye in the deep shadow of one of the pines near the parking lot. She was warm and we fit well in each other's arms. I could have stayed with her a lot longer, but she pushed away after a couple of minutes. "Maybe there's a big duffel bag to hide you."

"Just as long as it has air holes."

She looked serious. "I'd have to be really careful not to get caught slipping into it."

"That would be getting into the sack with me."

"You're terrible." She hugged me, then pushed away. "Enough. Back, beast! I'll see you in a week." She avoided a last embrace with a giggle and hurried off. "Say hello to your dad for me," she called.

I drove back to camp in the old pickup. Pete had let me fix it up and it was almost my personal vehicle for the summer—a real beater, but I could keep it going.

Dick was lying on his bunk reading a book. He reads more than anyone I've ever known. "Hi, Steve. Ed, the counselor from sixteen, dropped off a couple of cards for you. They were mixed in with the kids' mail. I put them on your bunk."

"Thanks."

He went back to reading.

The first card was from Mr. Ohm: "Thanks for the card with the view of the lake. Glad everything is going well. Pete wrote and said you were working out real good. Might get up some weekend fishing. Otherwise, see you in Capstone in the fall."

The other card was from Keith. "Nice lake you got, man. The carpentry program is good and one of the teachers hired me to help do some remodeling at his house in the evenings. Nothing too exciting—I mostly hold the idiot end of the boards, but it keeps me out of trouble. Write again. Take care, Keith."

Mel came in. "Hey, the great lover's back," he yelled. "A couple of the counselors are going into town. Want to come?"

"Sure," I said.

"Only if we don't have to ride in Steve's coffin," Dick said over the top of his book.

"Relax, Gramps, we'll take mine."

"Barely better," Dick muttered, but he levered himself up.

When I drove into Dad's campsite about nine o'clock on Saturday morning, I had a faint buzz in the back of my skull from the one or two too many beers I'd drunk at the bar in town where they don't check IDs real close. Dad came over to greet me. We shook hands.

"Hi, did you get set up okay?" I asked.

"Fine. No problems."

"Sorry I wasn't over to help earlier. Had a little trouble with the truck."

"No problem. That is some truck!"

"It's not bad, really. Still got a couple of bugs, but it runs better than it looks. How do you like the campsite?"

"Very nice. Thanks for reserving it." It was a nice spot—high atop a hill back from the lake with a breeze to keep off the insects. The campsites were well separated and the lake connected with several smaller lakes so you could fish all day without getting bored. I was proud of my choice.

"How about some coffee?" he asked.

"No, thanks. I'll take a Coke, though." He got me one and coffee for himself. We sat in the lawn chairs. Dad's idea of camping is to take all the luxury items: lawn chairs, charcoal grill, battery-operated TV, big tent, big cooler, boat, motor, and everything else he can pack in the boat, cram in the trunk, or lash atop the car.

"How's work going?" he asked.

"Good. About the same as when I called you last week."

"Are you enjoying the camp too?"

"It's okay. I had to put up a sign to keep the kids out of the shop, but no real problems."

We talked for half an hour. I told him about the activities and baby-sitting some of the kids at night if one of the counselors had a date and I didn't; about the guys I lived with and Pete; and about how much I liked the work and thought I was learning a lot.

He told me about going to dinner at Mattson's and how the

ol' hard ass seemed pretty good; about going fishing closer to home with Mr. Ohm; and so on. After a while he paused. "Steven, there's something I want to tell you. It's pretty big news. I'm giving up teaching."

I was stunned. "You are?"

He laughed softly. "I thought that would surprise you. Yes, I'm really going to. There's a job opening at the wildlife foundation lab over in Rutledge. They need someone to organize workshops and field trips. I interviewed for it on Tuesday and they hired me yesterday. Now don't panic. It's only eighteen miles and I'll commute, at least until you're out of school. You don't have to change any plans."

I was almost speechless. The Toad not teaching! "Well . . . congratulations, Dad!" I stuck out a hand.

Smiling broadly, he took it. "Thanks."

"But when do you start? And how about your pension? And won't you miss teaching?"

"Hold on. Hold on. I start September first. My pension benefits are secure and I'll actually be making a little more money. And I'll still be teaching some, but without a lot of the pressures. I'm a little tired of teaching high school. I've been doing it for over twenty years, and well, you know it's been kind of a strain the last couple of years. Time for a new beginning, I think."

"Dad, I couldn't be happier for you. Don't get me wrong, I think a lot of people will miss you, but well, I think you're right. You need a change."

He smiled, then reached over and slapped my knee. "Let's go fishing. I've got some sandwiches already made. We'll eat on the lake."

I got my pole and tackle box from the pickup and got in the Buick. He turned the key. The starter ground, the engine caught, labored, and died. He tried again. The engine caught again, chugged, coughed, and died. He tried again. The starter just ground. "Turn it off, Dad. It's not going anywhere."

We got out.

188

"I can't understand it. It was fine the other day," he said. I lifted the hood. This car hasn't been fine in two years, I thought. "Maybe it's the fan belt," he suggested.

I glanced at him. No, he wasn't kidding. "I doubt it, Dad." I pulled off the top of the air cleaner. The filter was solid black. "Didn't you have this tuned when you had the body repaired?"

"No, I didn't think it needed it."

I shook my head. What a mess! "I'm going to need some parts, Dad. Get a pad and a pen. You can use the pickup." I went to the truck for my toolbox.

It took me almost three hours to do a complete tune-up, including replacing the wires and distributor cap and changing the oil. Dad watched most of the process in silence. I suggested a couple of times that he go down to the lake and fish from shore, but he shook his head. "Won't catch much this time of day, anyway."

At last I finished. "Okay, Dad. Start her up."

The engine roared to life. I reached in and adjusted the idle, then stood back listening. Not bad.

"Sounds a lot better," Dad called.

"Ya. Lots better." I fiddled with the idle again. "Okay, shut it off." He did. "That's about as good as I can get it, Dad. I didn't have a timing light, so I guessed a little. The best thing to do is take it to a shop with a Sun machine and have them get it just right."

"A what?"

"A Sun machine, Dad. It's a tune-up machine." I explained.

When I'd finished, he stood with lips pursed. "You really like fixing cars, don't you?"

"Ya, I really do."

"Hmmm . . . I don't think I could ever get interested. Well, you seem to do it well."

"That was pretty simple."

"Well, after watching you work, I think I see things a little differently."

"How's that?"

"I guess I'd always thought you'd amount to something someday, but now I see you already do. You're a craftsman."

I started laughing. Well, I'll be damned. He'd finally noticed my true talents, such as they were. He looked a little confused, then started laughing too.

It was nearly one o'clock. He busied himself with getting out the sandwiches and stuff while I walked down to wash my hands at the restroom. When I was coming back up the path, Dad called, "Hey, the Brewers and the Twins are on at one. Want to watch the game? The fishing will be lousy until late afternoon."

"Whatever you want to do, Dad."

He turned on the game and we sat down to lunch.

Later we hauled the boat down to the lake and went on our long-delayed expedition. I watched him happily casting into the shallows. Wow. My dad, the infamous Toad, was actually giving up teaching. I shook my head. That'd be a big change for me too. Maybe people would even forget to call me Wart. Not that it really made much difference now. So many things that had once seemed very important now seemed very small.

I leaned back in my seat, lazily watching my line where it disappeared down in the deep green of the water. Let Dad work for the big one in the weeds. I was content to let the cool late-afternoon breeze wash the scent of pine over me.

Pacer

BOOKS FOR YOUNG ADULTS

__ **THE ADVENTURES OF A TWO-MINUTE WEREWOLF**
   by Gene DeWeese   0-425-08820-2/$2.50
When Walt finds himself turning into a werewolf, one two-minute transformation turns into a lifetime of hair-raising fun!

__ **FIRST THE GOOD NEWS**
   by Judie Angell   0-425-08876-6/$2.50
Determined to win the school newspaper contest, ninth-grader Annabelle Goobitz concocts a scheme to interview a TV star—with hilarious results!

__ **MEMO: TO MYSELF WHEN I HAVE A TEENAGE KID**
   by Carol Snyder   0-425-08906-1/$2.50
Thirteen-year-old Karen is sure her mom will never understand her—until she reads a diary that changes her mind...

__ **MEGAN'S BEAT**
   by Lou Willett Stanek   0-425-08416-7/$2.50
Megan never dreamed that writing a teen gossip column would win her so many friends from the city—or cost her so many from the farm!